A LOVE BEYOND

MARY'S LADIES, BOOK 2

BELLE MCINNES

Copyright © 2017 Belle McInnes
All rights reserved.
This book or any portion thereof may not be reproduced or used in any manner whatsoever without the express written permission of the publisher except for the use of brief quotations in a book review. You must not circulate this book in any format.
This book is a work of fiction. While reference might be made to actual historical events or existing locations, the characters, places and events are either the product of the author's imagination or are used fictitiously. Apart from well-known historical figures, any similarity to real persons, living or dead, is entirely coincidental.
This book is licensed for your personal enjoyment only.

Printed in the United Kingdom
First published, 2017
Cover by Alba Covers

Find out more about Belle and her upcoming books by joining her newsletter:
http://www.subscribepage.com/joinbelle

CONTENTS

ABOUT THIS BOOK

Mary Queen of Scots may reign, but her rivals will stop at nothing to gain the throne...

As handmaid to Mary Queen of Scots, heiress Libby Preston is in the perfect place to meet an eligible lord and make an advantageous marriage. But Libby is from the Borders of Scotland, where life is hard and lawless men run rampant. And this Borders lass has a terrible secret—a secret that would ruin her reputation and her chances of a suitable match, should it ever come to light...

French physician Robert Nau has come to Scotland to seek his fortune and work for the ageing ambassador in Edinburgh. He has no intention of falling in love—until he meets Libby Logan, a rich gentlewoman who is too highborn to consider man from his lowly background. But his heart yearns for her, even if their love is fated never to be.

When the queen falls mortally ill, Robert is sucked into the dramas and dangers of the Scottish court. Surrounded by ambitious men who seek their own advancement no matter the cost—even if that cost is regicide—he fights to heal the queen of a mystery ailment.

Working alongside Robert as the queen's fever worsens and she slips into unconsciousness, Libby finds it hard to deny her growing attraction to the handsome doctor. But she is destined to marry a Scottish lord, not a Frenchman from the slums of Paris;

and theirs is a match that can never be, a love
beyond reach…

MAP

SCOTLAND IN THE TIME OF MARY QUEEN OF SCOTS

CHAPTER 1

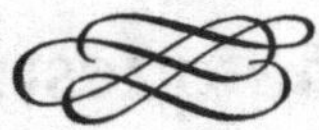

TUESDAY 8TH OCTOBER, 1566

"LOWER!" HISSED LORD Home, his dark green cape billowing behind him as he swept into a deferential bow.

With a grimace—which, due to her bowed head would thankfully not be seen by the queen—Libby Preston dropped her curtsey even lower. *My best dress! I shall never get the dust-stains removed from the hem.*

But her step-father had stressed the importance of impressing Mary, Queen of Scots, and gaining admittance to her court.

"We need to get you married to a suitable lord," Lord Home said last month, standing in the fire-lit solar of his castle at Hume in the Scottish Borders. "Or an earl—a duke is probably out of the question. But once you are advantageously wed, we need no longer worry about your—" he cleared his throat, "—little secret coming to light."

So here Libby was, wearing cramoisie silk, bedecked in her mother's second-best jewels and with her hair looped fashionably under a lace bonnet, almost on her knees before Mary Stuart in the great hall of Cowdenknowes Tower near Melrose, where Mary and her retinue had stopped en-route to Jedburgh.

"Good morrow, my lady Preston," said the queen with a lift of her hand.

Thankfully, Libby rose from her curtsey, and gave the monarch a shy smile. "They call me Libby, Your Grace," she replied, using the traditional Scots form of address for royalty.

A fire flickered in the gable wall, the spicy fragrance of burning wood mixing with the perfumed pomanders that scented the hall. On a long wooden table in the centre of the room, a platter of apples and pears sat invitingly. Libby's fingers itched to move the round plate, for it was not quite central on the oak board, and it offended her sense of order. But to do so would be considered rude, so she kept her fingers to herself.

Either side of the queen sat her ladies-in-waiting, known as 'the Maries'; for all four of them were also called Mary and had been brought up with the queen at the French court.

And that French influence was obvious in their clothing. Compared to the soberly dressed Scottish nobles, the Maries were bright and beautiful, like the iridescent tail-feathers of a peacock.

Wearing black as a mark of respect for her late husband, Francis the second of

France, the queen too embodied style and grace. With her garments of satin, taffeta and velvet, her gold enamelled jewellery and the stiff white ruff which emphasised the paleness of her face, she looked every inch a royal.

I must send off for more cloth and make some new dresses, thought Libby, clutching at the hidden pocket sewn into the lining of her gown, which contained a little purse of gold coin surreptitiously given to her by her mother. *None of my current wardrobe will do. For who will look at me, with the Maries to choose from?*

Although, was it not true that Mary Livingston and Mary Beaton were already married? So only Fleming and Seton were eligible. And Mary Seton had vowed eternal chastity, leaving only Mary Fleming as marriageable.

"I 'ear from Lord Home that you wish to join my court?" the queen continued.

"Yes, ma'am, I'd very much like to help you in any way I can."

Mary nodded graciously. "I am sure we could use another lady, for—" and here she looked sideways at the ladies-in-waiting who sat to either side of her, "two of my Maries are now wed, and will doubtless leave me once they are with child."

She touched the waves of auburn hair that framed her oval face, and nodded at the tall, fine-featured woman who sat to her left. "Mary Seton is gifted in dressing my 'air. Livvy—" the queen indicated the smaller lady next to Mary Seton, "Mary Livingston— looks after my jewellery. Beth Beaton assists me with my correspondence and reading, and Flam—Mary Fleming," here the queen's brow crinkled, and she added teasingly, "what *do* you do, Flam?"

Flam's blue eyes sparkled. "I keep you entertained, ma'am."

The queen lifted her eyebrows at her

handmaid. "Of course. How could I ever forget!"

Surreptitiously, Libby eyed Mary Fleming. With waves of dark hair, full lips and a curvaceous figure, she was beautiful in a dark, almost Italian way. Libby's figure was equally womanly, but her hair was the colour of heather honey, her skin creamy like finest asses' milk, and her eyes the grey-blue of a winter sky.

Mayhap I will be found attractive by different men. For not everyone will like her darkness. And she may not like the same men I do. Libby smoothed the voluminous skirts of her gown. *It only needs one.* And Libby had to find that man and make a prestigious marriage before the dark secret from her past came to light.

Near the studded oak entrance door stood a tall, fair-haired lord. He was handsome, although not to Libby's taste. But if she was not mistaken, Flam kept glancing across at him. And a greying, dignified gentleman who sat near to the queen could not take his eyes off the brunette. *So perchance she is already spoken for,* whichever side of the triangle might win. It did not mean that Libby would be sure to find a suitor here, but it might make it easier.

With a smile, the queen turned back to Libby. "And what talents do you 'ave to offer us, my dear?"

Libby took a deep breath. This was the decider. The answer that could affect her whole future. But she would answer truthfully, for any falsehood might leave her vulnerable to gossip, and she did not need to attract that kind of attention. "I enjoy needlework, ma'am. My stitch-work is neat and I love to work with fine fabrics. Could you use help with your wardrobe?"

Tuesday 1st October, 1566

Robert Nau almost snatched the letter from the liveried messenger's hand. "Merci, monsieur," he said with a voice gone suddenly hoarse.

Around him on the steps of the Hôtel-Dieu de Paris, people milled in and out of the hospital. Built in the year six-hundred and fifty-one on the bank of the Île de la Cité, one of the islands in the middle of the River Seine, Hôtel-Dieu was Paris' only hospital. Because of this, it was permanently busy, and always overflowing with needy patients.

As one of its junior physicians, Robert worked more hours than was healthy, often until he was so tired that he could hardly stagger back to the lodgings he shared with his brother.

But if this letter is what I think it is, my life will change forever. For the better. His heart hammering, Robert broke the seal and scanned the words scrawled on the ivory paper. A surge of joy flared in his chest. *Oui! It begins!*

Lifting his eyes to the north-west, he gazed over the soaring buttresses, squat towers and gothic spires of Notre Dame cathedral, and across the rooftops of the sprawling city, as if by some magic he might be able to see the distant shores of Scotland. For it was there that his future lay, in a post that would take him to castles and palaces—and possibly even into the presence of royalty.

Of course, he had heard of that fabled land; of its wild Highlanders, dark lochs and rugged hills. But he also knew that the wife of the previous French king was a Scottish princess; brought up in the French court and learning all the elegance and manners that went along with that. And now she was the Scots queen. So they could not *all* be heathens—a French-educated royal would never allow that.

It will be fine. It would be more than fine. It was his first step into aristocratic circles, and his chance to make a name for himself and leave behind the shame of his upbringing.

Beside him on the steps of the hospital, the messenger waited patiently for a reply. Taking a deep breath, Robert thrust the letter into the pocket of his leather jerkin and caught the man's eye. "D'accord. Tell him I accept. I shall come as soon as I can arrange passage."

~

Thursday 10th October, 1566

"Mon Dieu!" Mary's hand fluttered to her mouth and the letter she'd held fell to the table. *This changes everything.*

Her secretary, William Maitland of

Lethington, gave her a questioning look. A man whose grey hair, long face and solemn expression reflected his sober character, he was not the most entertaining company. But he was highly educated, and wise in the ways of court and the intrigues of politics. And she needed his advice more than ever, now.

"My lord Bothwell 'as been injured," she explained, "and lies gravely wounded at 'is castle near Castleton." After five years in Scotland, Mary's voice with its clipped vowels and lilting tone still gave a hint of her French upbringing. "And while 'e was out fighting with this Jock Elliot, the prisoners in 'is dungeon overcame their guards and would not admit the wounded earl to the castle unless 'e pardoned them all."

In her agitation, Mary couldn't sit still. A couple of steps took her to the small window in the first-floor room of the tolbooth tower, where she gripped the sill and stared unseeingly at the green hills on the far side of the Jed Water.

"So, there will be fewer people to judge at your assizes," Maitland summarised in his measured voice.

"Oui. But who will I get to help me? For Bothwell is my lieutenant of the Borders, and he knows the people here like no other." *And he is one of my few loyal lords, who I trust like no other. How will I manage without him?*

Maitland smoothed his beard with finger and thumb, taking a minute before he replied. "There is one here who might help. Young laird Cranstoun is deputy warden of the Middle March. And he seems to have a level head on his shoulders."

"Ah, oui." *The young lord I met yesterday. The one Lady Fleming was taken with.* "Yes, 'e will do. Send a message asking him to join us at the tolbooth." *Cranstoun will need to stay in Jedburgh for some days now.* Mary smiled to herself. *Flam will be pleased.*

It didn't take Libby long to settle into the routine of the Queen's household in Jedburgh. Sleeping in a tiny room in the garret, she would descend with the Maries shortly after dawn and break fast with the queen in the great hall on the first floor.

From there, Mary and some of her lords would go to the tolbooth where she held justice eyres. Her ladies would remain at the tower house, sewing, gossiping and playing cards.

Libby, more inclined to listen than talk, heard of Flam's regard for Michael Cranstoun, the deputy warden who assisted the queen with her assizes due to the injury sustained by her favourite, the earl of Bothwell.

"I saw him this morning," announced Flam, dark eyes sparkling, "riding his new horse along the river afore breakfast. A fine beast."

"The horse?" Livvy Livingston asked the obvious question.

Flam gave a coquettish look that belied her answer. "Of course. What else would I mean?"

Cranstoun was a laird with a castle, but no title, and as she unpicked a misaligned stitch, Libby found herself wondering at the confidence—or naivety—that would make Flam take interest in a man who could offer her neither money nor status. Perhaps Flam had such a large dowry that she did not need a rich husband? Or perhaps her family home never suffered attack by reivers intent on ill-gotten gains or kidnap for ransom?

The other side of that triangle, as observed by Libby on her first day, was the queen's secretary, William Maitland, an older, thin-faced man who made quiet suit to Mary Fleming.

To Libby's mind, the grey Maitland was a better prospect, with his prominent position at the queen's court and his large castle in East Lothian, which was a safer distance from the lawless border reivers than Libby's birthplace at Preston or her step-father's seat at Hume.

Whilst not discouraging Maitland, Flam made no secret of her admiration for Cranstoun, and seemed determined that she could marry for love, as had her friend Mary Livingston.

In contrast, Libby had no intention of following her heart. She needed the safety and security of an advantageous union, and had persuaded Lord Home that, rather than him arranging a marriage on her behalf, she should try a year at court as a lady-in-waiting. Mixing in the queen's circle, she might catch the eye of a greater lord than those of her step-father's acquaintance, and greater than her birthright deserved. So she had twelve months to find a noble lord and make him fall in love with her.

I will let my head rule my heart in this matter, for feelings should be put aside for the sake of the future. I will not be like Flam. As long as he is not an ogre I am sure I can respect any man and learn to suffer his company. Libby had known worse after all. Much worse.

~

Tuesday 1st October, 1566

Robert's brother smiled broadly and clasped his arms. "Beaucoup de félicitations! This is great news! Great news indeed."

"And all thanks to you, Claude," Robert replied. "If you had not spoken for me..."

At twenty-four, and younger than Claude by eight years, Robert had height and lean muscle where his brother was short and inclined to corpulence. If it wasn'tt for the brooding dark eyes and wide mouths they'd inherited from their mother, nobody would guess that they were brothers. *Or half-brothers*, Robert corrected himself. Despite the difference in their ages, they had been good friends in boyhood and grown even closer as adults, more-so than most full siblings. *I will miss him.*

"Nonsense!" His brother made a little flicking motion with his hand. "'Twas nothing. You were the premier student of your year at the university—"

"Which *you* paid for," Robert interrupted.

"Because I *could*. And I wanted *you* to have the same chances mother gave me. And see—it worked, for now you are top assistant to the renowned Monsieur Paré at Paris' only hospital. The ambassador would have been an imbecile to turn you down!"

Robert shrugged. "Mayhap he had no other applicants."

"Or mayhap he had no need of any others, once he saw the quality of your application." Claude looked his brother up and down, taking in the dark clothing that Robert customarily wore as it was less likely to show bloodstains and dirt. He pulled some gold coins from his pocket. "But please—go to my tailor and get yourself a new outfit before you go. You cannot go to Scotland looking like you've just come from a funeral." With a flourish, he indicated his slashed satin doublet, cambric shirt and pan velvet hose. "We need to show them that France still has the best fashions in Europe, as well as the best wine," he put a hand on his brother's back and grinned, "and the best physicians."

Guiding Robert towards the door, Claude added, "Now, come. A new tavern has opened near Les Halles. Chez Havard, they call it. I hear their cellar is excellent and their kitchens even better. Let me help you celebrate!"

CHAPTER 2

SUNDAY 6TH OCTOBER, 1566

TURNING EAST TO face into the rising sun, Robert's feet slapped on hardened dirt as he ran down the narrow streets. With his shoulders back and his head high, he pumped his arms in time with his long strides. Today, his route skirted the marketplace of Les Halles, where the stall-keepers unloaded their pungent and colourful wares and shouted cheerful greetings at one another.

Usually Robert enjoyed his early morning runs, with the chance to see the city before it was fully awake, sparkling in the golden light of dawn. With its dirt and seedier corners hidden in the shadows, you could almost believe that Paris was a city where angels might live.

But Robert's work at Hôtel-Dieu had opened his eyes to the squalid underbelly that haunted every district; to the crime, poverty and depravity that lived just below the city's veneer of elegance and respectability.

His desire to help others, to heal their sicknesses and bind their wounds, had sustained him this far, and his faith had kept his heart hopeful despite all the terrible things he'd seen. But it was time for a change. Time for a new challenge in a new country. His soul needed it. *He* needed it. And the things he learned in Scotland—and the money he earned—would allow him to come back to Paris in a few years and open his own hospital, where he could make a *real* difference.

This new life started today, in just a couple of hours. After he attended Mass at the cathedral, Robert would eat with his brother for one last time before meeting the guards the ambassador had sent to accompany him. Then they would ride for Le Havre and the barque that would take him to Scotland and his new employment as physician to the French ambassador. But it meant saying farewell to this flawed but addictive city, his work at the hospital, and his brother —for a time at least.

So this last run through the city evoked bittersweet emotions. But he needed it. He needed the clarity of mind, the buzz in his muscles, and the lift in his spirits that running gave him. It was like a drug, but one that cost nothing and made his body stronger and fitter. He couldn't understand why more people didn't try it.

It was when Robert ran around the last corner of the market that things took a turn for the worse. Blocking his path were two swarthy men in tattered dark clothing who smelled as evil as they looked.

With a murmured, "Excusez-moi," Robert stepped to the left to continue his run.

The taller man caught his right arm. "Not so fast, monsieur."

The glint of a knife in the other miscreant's hand had Robert reacting without thinking. Tensing his stomach muscles, he grabbed onto the man's forearm and swung him off-balance, crashing him into his friend. It was enough to gain the release Robert needed, and with a kick of his heels he was sprinting away down Rue des Halles.

However, the would-be robbers didn't give up. With a growl, they set off in pursuit, lumbering along after Robert with a great huffing and puffing and flapping of their filthy jerkins. But their chase didn't last long. Robert's fit body and regular training meant that he could easily out-run them, both on distance and speed, and he quickly lost sight of them.

At the corner of Rue de Rivoli he stopped briefly and checked behind him, his chest heaving but a grin on his face. The street was empty. *My morning run is not usually so exciting!* It pleased him, though, for his escape proved the value of the exercise he did on a daily basis.

Starting off again—at a slower pace this time—he carried on down the wide avenue with its views over the Palais du Louvre, the king's residence in the city.

With its grand facades and opulent interiors, the palace spoke of wealth and power —which was surely the intent—but it didn't impress Robert. For he knew that the rich needed the ministrations of a doctor almost as often as the poor, even if for different ailments. And he knew that their lives were no more perfect. A noble was as likely to die or be killed by power-mongering, poison or jealousy as the lower classes were to die from crime, hunger and hardship.

People were the same all over. It was just their situations that were different. And Robert could help and heal them—*would* help and heal them, whoever they were.

~

Thursday 10th October, 1566

James Hepburn, Earl of Bothwell and Queen's Lieutenant of the Borders lay on his bed and groaned with frustration. For the second time in as many days his physician had bled him. But, despite these ministrations, the scar on his forehead ached so he could hardly think straight, his lacerated hand felt like it held a fiery poker, and the wound in his side flamed red and angry like a blacksmith's forge.

By now the queen would be in Jedburgh, holding her assizes. *I should have been by her side.* But his injuries confined him to his bed; his doctor recoiling in horror any time Bothwell as much as mentioned sitting up.

Who will take my place? Who will she ask to guide her as she passes judgement? The earl's jaw clenched. *As long as 'tis not Moray. The queen puts too much stock in that wily fox.*

With an imperious finger he beckoned his manservant, Nicholas Hubert, more commonly known as 'French Paris'. *I will find out.* "Paris," he said, "ride to Jedburgh and find out who presides at the assizes with the queen. Find out how much influence Moray has, and whether Maitland whispers in her ear."

Mayhap if I know what I deal with, I can make a plan to restore my position. He ground his teeth. *Once I am recovered.* "Damn Jock Elliot," he muttered, not caring who heard, "damn his black soul to hell and back!"

His skin tingling from the cold water he'd splashed on his face, Robert straightened from the trough in the stable yard and wiped his eyes. *If only it was as easy to wipe the fatigue from my brain.* Even the reek of the midden wasn't enough to reach through the fog of tiredness that muddied his thoughts and dulled his movements.

Not far from the timbered walls of the inn where he'd spent the night, the soaring spires of Rouen's great Notre Dame cathedral reached for the sky like the grasping fingers of a dying man reaching for heaven.

One of these spires, he'd been told, was called the 'Butter Tower'; having been built from the fines levied on rich burghers who could not forgo the indulgence of butter during Lent. But it was that self-same Butter Tower that was the cause of his tiredness.

Once each hour through the longest night he'd ever known a bell had pealed, waking him from fitful sleep and nonsensical dreams.

Eventually, in the grey hours before dawn, he gave up and lay staring at the heavy wooden beams of the ceiling until footsteps creaking down the stair outside his room told him that it was time to get up, break fast with his guards and continue their journey to the coast.

If the citizens of Rouen hadn't loved their butter so much, Robert might not have been so tired, and he might have noticed the shadowy figures flitting through the trees beside their path through the Maulévrier forest.

Without butter, he might have had time to draw his sword, or warn the guards who ambled ahead of him on their broad-backed ponies.

Instead, when three masked men burst from the trees with doglock rifles cocked and murder in their eyes, Robert and his companions were caught unawares.

"Halt!" cried the lead highwayman—unnecessarily, for the sight of three strange men on horseback had stopped their horses in their tracks, nostrils flaring and necks tense.

The would-be robber motioned with the muzzle of his gun. "Dismount. Keep yer hands where we can see 'em."

In front of him, the guards swung gingerly from their mounts, and Robert followed their example, his heart hammering and all his senses—at last, despite his sleepless night—primed for action.

One musket remained trained on Robert's little band whilst two of the highwaymen, guns tucked securely under their arms, proceeded to pat them down and search their saddlebags.

They found slim pickings—until they noticed the wooden valise strapped to the back of Robert's saddle. "What 'ave we 'ere?" demanded the younger brigand, heaving at the heavy case.

But the pack was securely tied, and at the highwayman's rough handling, Robert's horse spooked, swinging its quarters away from the robber and clattering into one of the guard's ponies.

Briefly, the restless horses shielded Robert from the lead highwayman, and he leapt into action. Stepping close to the young brigand, he jabbed his elbow at the vulnerable spot on the man's temple with as much force as he could muster.

Like a tree felled by lightning, the thief crashed to the ground, and one of Robert's guards, taking his cue from the doctor, ducked low, pulled a dagger from his boot and swung it at the second robber.

By this time Robert had grabbed the rifle from the lifeless man at his feet, dodged round the horses and pointed the gun at the lead highwayman. "Drop your weapon!"

With both of Robert's guards approaching him menacingly, and a gun trained at his head, the miscreant did not tarry. Swinging his horse around, he dug his spurs into its sides and raced away, leaving his companions to their fate.

"Get him," shouted one of the guards, pointing at Robert's musket.

Robert expelled the air from his lungs, narrowed his eyes and aimed at the retreating man's back. Squeezing the trigger, he was momentarily blinded by the puff of gunpowder, and deafened by the roar of the explosion. But his shot went wide, and the highwayman galloped away unhindered. *A cheap weapon. The sight is off.*

"Shall I chase him, sire?" asked one of the guards.

Robert shook his head, rubbing his shoulder where it stung from the recoil. "Check the other two."

A toe prodded the youth Robert had felled. "This 'un's dead."

But a groan from the masked figure who lay curled up on the dirt track proved that the other had survived. Blood seeped from a wound in his gut, the man's fingers bright red as they pressed his side in an effort to staunch the flow.

"Get my valise!" Robert ordered, turning the man onto his back and ripping open his jerkin. "And give me your water skin," he demanded of the other guard.

"Why not just finish 'im off?" the guard asked.

Robert shook his head. "Every man deserves a chance—the chance to repent of his crimes and turn over a new leaf." Pouring water on the gash to clean it, Robert packed moss over the wound then bound it tight with a bandage. "Tie his hands," he instructed when he'd finished, "and sit him on one of their horses. We'll take him to the magistrate in the next town."

"You heal him, just for him to face the noose?" The guard scratched his bulbous nose, thick eyebrows almost meeting in the middle.

"Oui. But if he makes his peace with God, this man may yet have a chance of heaven." Robert mounted his horse. "'Tis all that any of us can ask."

I n these first days in Jedburgh, Libby merely observed, rather than showing her hand. She took note of who was in the queen's favour, and who had influence with the other lords. It became apparent that most of Mary's advisors were older—and married. *But they will have sons, who might do me very nicely. Or be widowed.* All was not lost.

The formality of dinner in the royal

household aided in her endeavours. When the business at the tolbooth had finished for the day, Mary would return, perhaps take a walk in the gardens, and then change for the evening repast.

At dinner, the most important nobles would be seated nearest the queen. Libby sat with the Maries and some of the lesser lords —such as laird Cranstoun—at a lower table. But it put her in the perfect position to note who was in favour, who made the queen laugh, and who had her hanging on their every word.

However, the fact that Libby sat quietly and kept in the background did not stop her catching the eye of Hugh, Master of Somerville, eldest son and heir of Lord Somerville, one of Mary's parliamentary lords. After dinner on her second night, Hugh stopped by their table and had Beth Beaton introduce him to 'their lovely new friend'.

Libby greeted him politely, noting the fine cut of his surcoat and the roundness of his moon-face. But then he was pulled away to talk to the earl of Atholl.

The next evening, the air was crisp and clear, and Flam suggested a walk in the dark, up to the ruined castle. "Mayhap we shall see the ghost of some English prisoner," she said with a lift of her shoulder.

Livvy Livingston pursed her lips. "Or mayhap the shadow of some cutpurse intent on relieving us of our jewels."

"Nonsense!" Flam indicated Laird Cranstoun and Sir Thomas Kerr of Ferniehirst who sat with them. "The gentlemen will keep us safe."

Cranstoun held up his hands. "Count me out, ladies. 'Twas a long day at the courts, and I've reading to do, to prepare for the morn." He gave a small bow in Flam's direction. "My apologies."

Flam's mouth turned down at the corners, and she was about to say something when a deep voice rumbled from behind Libby.

"I can accompany you, if you wish," said Hugh Somerville. "With Sir Thomas, we shall be two swords to protect you." He swivelled his eyes to the top table. "Maitland might be persuaded to join us too."

And so it was that Libby found herself strolling through the darkened streets of Jedburgh with the young Master Somerville by her side, enjoying the bite of the crisp autumn air and admiring the infinite blackness of the star-spangled sky.

"Are you Lord Hume's only daughter?" Hugh asked after a few moments, his voice booming through the quiet streets like the bellow of a hungry bull.

Glancing across at him, she tried not to show annoyance that he'd interrupted her meditation. "His *step*-daughter. My mother is his second wife."

"Oh. So your father is…?"

"*Was*," she corrected, then continued. "Robert Logan of Restalrig."

"My father is James, Lord Somerville," he said, as if she didn't know. "And our family seat is Couthally Castle in Lanarkshire. The Queen visited us three years ago. She said she enjoyed the hawking. And she was impressed by our herd of beef cattle."

Libby nodded politely, although because of the darkness he probably couldn't see.

"Our lands at Carnwath are extensive." He glanced sideways at her, so Libby tried to look impressed. "But we have a factor who manages the estate. Which leaves me free to accompany my father to parliament, or to hunt, or," he peered across at her again, "to attend the queen and her ladies at court."

Their route through the town had taken them up to castle hill, a grassy mound with the tumbled remains of thick walls and a magnificent view over the town. The musty scent of sandstone was brought to them by the same light breeze that scattered a few dry leaves and sent them skittering down the hill towards the marketplace. All around them were shadowy hills, and below, the dark, wooded valley of the Jed Water stretched north to south like black velvet binding on a mourning dress.

Beside her, Hugh was still talking about his herds and crops. *Farmer John,* she thought to herself, then tuned him out again as she drew closer to the others, who had also stopped to admire the view. When Somerville stopped talking for a moment to draw breath, she intervened with a question. "Did the English demolish the castle?"

"I believe so—"

"Nay," Sir Thomas interrupted. "'Twas the Scots. The English had occupied it so often that Balvenie had it razed so that they could no longer gain a stronghold in our area."

"A desperate measure," Libby commented.

"True. But in times of war, men often have to resort to the unthinkable," Ferniehirst replied. "And our borderlands have been crossed by armies so often that if you cannot build a fortified house, there is almost no point in building at all."

"So that is why the homes of the common folk are so poor?"

"Aye. And they fear to plant and grow, for an army marches on its stomach, and their crops seldom last through to harvest."

It was something she'd never really thought about before, but it explained a lot about the land she'd grown up in, and the men who had attacked Preston Tower that awful night last November. "Is that why they reive?"

Sir Thomas nodded. "On a winter's night when the bairns are hungry and the last tup has been slaughtered for meat, they'll go in search of another's flocks to feed their children."

"You sound like you have some sympathy for them, young Kerr!" Hugh clapped him on the shoulder.

Sir Thomas grimaced. "Not sympathy so much as understanding." He pointed south-east down the valley. "Our own castle was occupied by the English in fifteen forty-seven, during the Rough Wooing. We only gained it back with the help of some French mercenaries. Hartrigge House, where the queen is staying," he nodded at Mary, who stood nearby, conversing quietly with William Maitland, "my grandfather built at the command of James the fifth who wanted more fortified dwellings to help withstand the English. Things in the Borders have never been easy—and it's not just the English, for the Scots army marches south as often as the English come north. We are like a pantry for the quartermasters, and the first place where the English may claim a victory in any campaign. 'Tis a hard life, being a Marchman."

For the first time in her nineteen years, Libby began to understand a little of what might have driven the Herons to attack Preston Tower, and do the terrible things they'd done. She could not excuse them—could never excuse them—but she could see why they might think they had reason. "But how can they live with themselves, the reivers? And gamble on escaping the courts." Libby gestured down at the town. "Pity knows the queen has been kept busy these last days. Why would they break the law and risk the noose?"

"When you have nothing, you will try anything. For how much lower can you go?"

Very true, thought Libby. Risking everything was something she knew all about, for that described exactly what she herself was doing here in Jedburgh, venturing her reputation and her future in an attempt to allay the misfortunes of the past. *Mayhap I'm a reiver too. But not a reiver that steals cattle, one that looks to win a heart...*

~

Monday 14th October, 1566

Standing at the side of the three-masted merchant ship as it sailed up the Firth of Forth towards the port of Leith, Robert shivered and pulled his cloak tighter around his shoulders. Scotland was notice-ably colder than France, the chill wind whistling along the deck and filling the canvas with a whip-like crack, causing ropes to strain and masts to creak.

Leaning his elbows on the rail, he gazed at the unfamiliar shoreline of his new home. All along this coast of the estuary, flat land rolled from the sea towards a ridge of low hills some miles to the south. At a few strategic points, he could see the dark shapes of stone towers, presumably built for defence—or lookout.

From the history he'd studied, Robert knew that it was not unknown for English armies to march through southern Scotland, for they had long had designs on annexing Scotland. When the current Scots queen, Mary Stuart, was younger and unmarried, King Henry the eighth of England had tried to get her betrothed to his young son, Edward, in an attempt to join the crowns. And when the Scots nobles and Mary's mother, acting as Regent, had resisted Henry's suggestions, he'd sent his armies north, razing the area around Edinburgh in what the Scots had ironically called the 'rough wooing'.

But it was all to no avail—for the Scots thumbed their noses at the English king by sending Mary to the safety of France, engaging her to the young dauphin, Francis the second.

These Scots sound like they have a sense of humour, Robert thought. *But I will soon be able to judge for myself.* For the ship drew closer to the shore, the harbour walls enticing it closer like the arms of a lover waiting to circle it in their embrace.

Robert raised his gaze and examined the area beyond the smoky buildings huddled around the port of Leith. In the middle distance rose a lumpen hill, crouched like a sleeping lion waiting to pounce on what must be Edinburgh castle, perched at the top of a rocky escarpment close by. Crowded around the castle was the city of Edinburgh, inside its tall stone walls.

But that city was *very* different to his native Paris. Considerably smaller, for a start, and with no river Seine cutting it in two. The countryside was closer though. *Perhaps I'll be able to run through woods and fields, rather than along dusty city streets.* He had heard that the ambassador joined the Scots court in hunting and hawking on occasion, and with parkland and woods so close by, he could see why.

Drawing alongside the dock, sailors scurried to make the ship fast, winding thick hawsers around solid stanchions, furling canvas and securing the gangplank. Robert's excitement grew, as did his relief that this voyage, which had seemed interminable on the first day when bad weather plagued them, had reached its end.

It was ironic that he, a physician, should have suffered so badly from seasickness, and been unable to help himself. But eventually his body had acclimatised to the constant rolling motion of the North Sea, and, as the weather had improved, so had his demeanour.

Mayhap when I return to France, I should ride south to the English ports, rather than taking such a long journey by sea. It was a difficult decision, choosing between the dangers of piracy and sickness at sea, and the risk of highway robbery on the longer land journey. *But that is a choice for another time, another year.* First, he had to make his way in this new land, working for a new master.

~

Robert had seldom been so thankful as he was when his feet finally touched dry land for the first time in days. Standing on the stone wharf in Leith as seamen bustled around him, unloading, unfurling and securing, he took a deep breath of the briny air and turned his face to the south.

"Robert Nau?" asked a short, grey-haired man at his elbow.

"Oui. Ah, I mean, yes," Robert replied, remembering that he had to speak *English* now, even though he was in Scotland.

The newcomer doffed his hat and gave a stiff bow. "I'm Édouard McMann. I've been sent by Monsieur du Croc the ambassador. He's waiting for you in Edinburgh." Mc-Mann flicked a finger at a horse and cart standing by some barrels of pickled herring. "We can load your things and they'll follow us up. He's sent a horse for you. You *do* ride?" he added anxiously.

Robert touched the brim of his hat and nodded. "Yes. But my trunk is not yet unloaded."

For some minutes, they watched as, with practised efficiency, the deck hands carried crates, sacks and trunks down the narrow gangway, balancing their awkward burdens as if they weighed no more than a small child. At last, Robert's luggage appeared, and within minutes they were on their way southwards through the grimy streets of the small town.

McMann turned out to be the ambassador's secretary, born in Scotland but to a French mother, so bi-lingual. During the short journey, he appraised Robert of the composition of the ambassador's household. "And we're about to go south. To the borderlands—Jedburgh. Her Grace is holding assizes there." At Robert's puzzled look, he added, "Justice courts. Eyres, we call them."

So he would meet the queen. *How my life has changed.*

CHAPTER 3

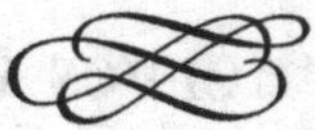

TUESDAY 15TH OCTOBER, 1566

'Twas the final day of the assizes, and all was a-bustle in the queen's tower house, for the French Ambassador, Philibert du Croc, had arrived in the small Borders town, and Mary was hosting an afternoon reception for him.

"My new dress," she commanded when she returned from the tolbooth. "The one with the pearls—Libby, can you get it pressed and ready? Ebba," she turned to Mary Seton, nicknamed after the ninth-century saint of chastity, "will you dress my 'air

49

for the satin and pearl bonnet? And Livvy, the black enamelled necklace set from my trunk."

Her ladies rushed in all directions while Mary steadied her nerves with a small goblet of sack. Today had been a fraught day at the court, her half-brother Moray castigating her for clemency while the poor miscreants arrayed before her told stories of hardship and trouble which made her heart weep. How could things be so terrible for her people, here in the Marches? Were it not for the English and their continual attempts to annex Scotland, there would be peace, and the Borderers could grow their crops and tend their cattle without fear of invasion.

I shall write my cousin Elizabeth again, she decided. *Entreat her once more to name my son as her heir, so our lands will be joined under one king. That is the only way to bring peace to the borders.* Elizabeth had stone-walled her until now, still angry that Mary had chosen to marry Henry Darnley—a Catholic who also had a claim to the English throne—rather than Elizabeth's favourite, Robert Dudley. But Elizabeth was famously a virgin—or at least, she *said* she was; court gossip had it otherwise—with no intention of marrying and sharing her crown with any man.

Given the trouble Mary was having with her husband Darnley and his demands for the crown matrimonial, Mary had some sympathy for Elizabeth's position. But a virgin queen would need an heir, and who better than the son of her cousin in Scotland, bringing peace to her realm? For the northern counties of England suffered from reiving and invasion as much as did the southern counties of Scotland. *Peace will benefit us all. I shall write tonight.*

Rushing around to prepare the queen to meet the ambassador, Libby had little time to think about her own outfit. But for such an important dignitary, she should surely wear her best dress, the cramoisie? The new one she was making from the sapphire satin she'd ordered using the gold coin from her mother was not ready yet; she still had to add lace to the bodice and more gold embroidery to the skirts. But the blue was more modern, more in keeping with what she had learned of French fashion from the other ladies. *I shall try it on and then decide.*

Standing in her tiny room in the attic, she turned this way and that, trying to catch sight of her reflection in the glass of the window. Without the lace to edge the bodice, her décolletage was on proud display; more revealing than was her normal style. *But is it not the French way?* Would it honour the ambassador to wear such a dress? Or would it attract the wrong kind of attention? She chewed her lip.

If she was quick, there was still time to stitch on some lace and preserve her modesty. But like this it made her feel more womanly. More powerful. With her essence hidden, but hinted at; with *her* in control of what showed, and what remained hidden. *And I have lots to hide.* But nobody else need know that. *Perhaps a dress like this will make me seem more open, more obvious? And more likely to attract a rich lord?*

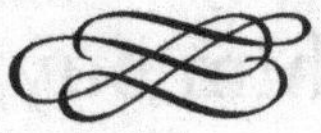

CHAPTER 4

ROBERT AND McMANN followed the ambassador, Philibert du Croc, up the turnpike stair of the Jedburgh tower house where the queen had her lodgings. From above came the sounds of music and animated chatter, and Robert's stomach fluttered with excitement.

Breathing heavily, the ambassador stopped to catch his breath. "They say the spiral turns to the left," he wheezed, "because it was built by the left-handed Kerrs of Ferniehirst, and would give them an advantage when fighting any right-handed attackers."

Nodding sagely, Robert pulled at the front of his new doublet—part of the outfit Claude had made him buy; a thing of extravagance rather than practicality. But he was glad of it now, for he could not meet the queen of Scots looking like he'd just stepped from a Parisian sickroom.

The slashed velvet jerkin and woollen hose were not in his customary black, but instead in a deep, rich brown that was so dark it reminded him of the Parisian sky at midnight. Gold bound the cut edges of the jerkin, gold piping decorated the collar, and gold buttons held the front edges together. Underneath, he wore a slashed and pinked satin doublet over a fine cambric shirt with lace ruffles at the neck and cuffs, both in a creamy-white which complemented his olive-toned skin and dark hair. It was the best that Claude's tailor could produce in the few days before Robert met with the ambassador's guards for the journey to Le Havre, and while it was of sober design compared to the rakish excesses of the French court, it was as fancy as Robert could be comfortable with. He preferred plain, but it appeared that French tailors didn't *do* plain.

Straightening, Monsieur du Croc lifted his chin towards the final flight of stone steps leading to the first-floor banqueting hall. "Remember, address the queen as 'Your Grace' the first time you meet her. And only speak once she has spoken to you."

Robert nodded again. "Oui. Of course."

"She doesn't stand too much on ceremony, for those she likes, and those in her inner circle. But'tis best to conform to etiquette when first introduced." Du Croc raised an eyebrow. "We wouldn't want to ruffle the diplomatic waters. Now," he started up the stairs again, "come and meet the queen of Scots."

Standing to the right of Flam and Maitland who attended the queen at the far end of the banqueting hall, Libby was in prime position to observe the ambassador and his attendants as they opened the heavy oak door and stepped into the room.

Heels tapping across the polished floor, the ambassador crossed the room, removed his hat, and bowed low before the queen, velvet robes flowing around his knees. A stout man with a guarded face, pointed beard and hair that was more reminiscent of salt than pepper, he greeted the queen in French. "Enchantée, majesté."

Behind him came a middle-aged, plain-faced man wearing eyeglasses, and then a young man who was so handsome, the sight of him stopped the breath in Libby's throat, and sucked all the air from the room. For a moment, she thought she might swoon.

Tall, olive-skinned and dark-haired, he wore a dashing outfit of rich brown, gold and cream, which emphasised his lean frame and powerful muscles. But it was his smile as he bowed before the queen that bewitched Libby. Wide and unaffected, his full lips twitched up at the corners, making his brown eyes sparkle with warmth and a hint of mischief. *Here is a lord whose heart I might wish to win.*

With a flourish, the ambassador introduced his companions to the queen. "Your Grace, may I present to you my secretary, Monsieur Édouard McMann, and my physician, Monsieur Robert Nau."

Or not a lord. Libby's shoulders drooped. Here stood the first man who had quickened her pulse since she arrived at court, and he had no title. Was this the way it was to be? That the only eligible lord to take an interest in her would bore her to tears, and anyone who made her heart sing would be unavailable to her?

In comparison to Monsieur Nau, whose expression almost glowed with curiosity and intelligence, Hugh Somerville's moon face seemed pasty, lifeless and bland. *But he will be the seventh lord of Somerville one day, and laird of Couthally castle. I must keep my purpose in mind.* With a heavy sigh, she turned her attention back to the queen.

~

Rising from his bow, Robert gazed with admiration at the queen. She was beautiful, like he'd been told. Tall—taller than usual for a woman, and taller than many men—she carried herself with graciousness and elegance. *As I'd expect from one brought up in France.* Auburn hair framed an oval face with perfect white skin, fine lips and expressive green eyes.

And those eyes crinkled at the corners as

the queen greeted them. "Bonsoir, gentle-men," she said, and swept an arm around the room. "The court of Scotland welcomes you. Please make yourselves known to my lords and ladies. Refreshments will be served mo-mentarily."

Murmurs of conversation began to fill the air as, from a doorway in the far corner of the room, liveried servants appeared bearing trays of wine and sweetmeats.

Robert took this opportunity to scruti-nise the soberly dressed men and more colourful ladies arrayed around the ban-queting hall.

Most of the men were older, and some eyed the ambassador from under lowered brows. *Mayhap these are the Protestant lords McMann told me about.* Nearer the queen stood her ladies, some of whom rivalled the monarch herself in looks and finery. But it was the younger fair-haired maid to the left of the queen who caught his eye. With hair the colour of spun gold, a heart-shaped face and lips that could grace a cherub, she wore a stunning—and daring—blue gown that emphasised the azure of her eyes.

"Welcome to Scotland, Monsieur Nau," said a husky voice at his elbow, tearing his attention away from the beautiful maid. "I am Mary Fleming—or Flam, as most call me." Her eyes flashed at him in an unspoken signal that he read as easily as he read his medical textbooks. *She flirts with me.* On another day, he might have found himself taken with her full figure and dark looks. But compared to the intriguing blonde she seemed brazen and obvious.

He kissed her hand. "A pleasure to meet you, mademoiselle."

Flam fluttered her eyelashes at him, then indicated a white-haired, black-eyed man behind her, with a face whose red nose and thready veins bespoke of a penchant for alcohol. "Monsieur Jacques Lusgerie, the queen's physician, wanted to meet you. I am sure you will have much to talk about."

"Delighted to make your acquaintance." Robert clasped the older man's hand, but his grip was limp, like a half-dead fish.

"You studied in Paris?" Lusgerie asked, without preamble.

"Oui. Under André Vésale, God rest his soul. You knew him?"

"Only by reputation." Lusgerie's lips narrowed. "I don't have time for new-fangled ideas like his." He crossed his arms on top of his ample paunch. "For over twenty years I've been physician to the queen—since her childhood in France—and I've had little need of anything save bloodletting and purging."

Robert kept his expression neutral. "Her Grace must value your experience."

Flam intervened. "We should not monopolise you, Monsieur Lusgerie." She caught Robert's eye and lifted her chin in the direction of the other ladies. "Let me introduce you to my friends."

A moment later, Robert found himself inclining his head before the fair-haired beauty, who Flam introduced as Lady Libby Logan of Preston.

"Enchantée, Mademoiselle Logan," he said, taking her hand, pleased to notice a catch in her breath at his touch. Holding her gaze, he bent his lips to her fingers, marvelling at how this slightest of contacts made his skin tingle and his pulse race. *Does she feel it too?* As he straightened and reluctantly dropped her hand, colour rose in her cheeks, giving him his answer. *Oui.*

Before Flam presented him to the next lady, Robert found his mind wandering, dreaming about what it might be like to get to know Libby better, to hold her, caress her, kiss her… and to give her pleasure in the ways he had learned while growing up in Paris. For he had understood from an early age that women deserved to be cherished, adored and satisfied; and he had been taught by the ladies at his mother's establishment that the man who would unselfishly seek their enjoyment before his own would ultimately gain a far bigger bounty than his imagination could ever conjure. What would it be like, to win the heart of a maid such as Libby?

And then reason reasserted itself.

This comely Scottish mademoiselle, however beautiful and tempting she might be, was a noble lady, and out of reach to one such as him. He needed to remember his place, and his purpose here. He needed to build his reputation and his fortune, so that he could help the deserving people of his hometown. And so he needed to forget any foolish notion of loving a Scots noblewoman, for it would get him nowhere, and drive him to madness in the process.

CHAPTER 5

WEDNESDAY 16TH OCTOBER 1566

DESPITE HIS RESOLUTION to forget his attraction to Libby, at first light the next morning, Robert found himself mounted on a black horse and riding alongside the woman who had filled his dreams and kept him tossing and turning through the hours of darkness on his straw mattress in the tiny room he shared with McMann at their lodgings near Jedburgh's marketplace.

Somehow, during the reception last

night, he had been invited to join the royal party in an expedition to some distant castle so that the queen could meet with her lieutenant of the Borders. It was Flam's doing, most likely, for he remembered her saying that he should be given the opportunity to explore the Scottish countryside, and learn more of their ways. This last was said with a coquettish smile that only served to emphasise the double meaning of her words.

But this morn—which had dawned so grey and misty that he would see little of the scenery they rode through—Flam rode with the blond laird whose castle they were to visit first. *Mayhap she has realised that I have no interest in her*, Robert thought with relief.

For just as Libby was beyond his reach, the high-born Flam would also never consider a commoner such as he. Or at least, not as a husband. She might countenance a dalliance with a man who could… *entertain* her. But such a man could never aspire to be more than an object of desire, sneaking along corridors at dead of night, or stealing furtive embraces in darkened corners that would hide the illicit lovers from discovery and gossip.

And Robert had no desire merely to warm the bed of a woman who would surely calculate the advantages of a potential marriage with the same calculating gaze she used to appraise his long legs and muscular chest.

If he were ever to marry—and it was not something that featured in his current plan—it would be to a French lass who would help him with the hospital and not look at him with disdain when she learned of his shameful upbringing.

But in the meantime, there was no reason he could not be polite to his travelling companion. It would help the journey pass more quickly, and mayhap Libby could teach him something of this land they rode through, which was as different from France as night from day.

~

Riding west towards Stobs Castle on her chestnut palfrey, every fibre of Libby's being was intensely aware of the Frenchman who rode alongside her, favouring her with his smile and attending every word she spoke as if it were the wisdom of Solomon, rather than the simple utterings of a Scottish lass.

And that in itself was something of a miracle. For Libby, never one to speak any more than she had to, was being drawn out by his gentle questions and genuine interest in what she thought, and where she lived, and what she'd done.

He asked her about her childhood, about her upbringing in Preston tower and her learning from the tutor employed to educate her brother. He asked about life here in the Borders of Scotland, and about the reivers that the queen judged at the assizes. He asked about her work with the queen and the activities that filled her days. He seemed genuinely interested in *her*, and what she felt and thought, unlike any man she had come across thus far in her short life.

When he discovered that she liked clothes, and made her own gowns, she was finally able to turn the tables on him, quizzing him about the ladies of France and the latest fashions in dresses and bonnets. She made him describe the colours, the cuts, the fabrics; how the gowns were trimmed and laced, how they wore their hats and how they styled their hair.

"You are so fortunate!" she exclaimed when she finally seemed to have exhausted his knowledge of French couture. "To be able to see it all at first-hand. I would so love to…" and then the words dried in her throat.

She had been about to say how she would love to visit France. *But that will seem like I encourage him. And I cannot. He is a mere physician, and I need to marry a lord.*

With a tilt of her chin, she changed the subject. "But look! We are nearly there." Guiding her horse along a narrow path through a dense forest that smelled of peat and decay, teasing glimpses of stone battlements appeared between the golds and browns of the autumnal trees. "Is that not our destination ahead?"

After a short break for breakfast, they left Stobs Castle to travel the remainder of the distance to Hermitage. But Robert was disappointed to see Libby's chestnut alongside the fine horses of the other ladies. *I will have to do without her company for this leg of our journey, it seems.*

Pushing his horse up to the front, where he would get a better view of the scenery they would pass, Robert rode alongside Laird Cranstoun and Sir Thomas Kerr, who led the group.

The weather had cleared a little now, and he gazed in awe at the rugged hills and broken valleys of the Scottish borderland. The landscape was desolate and primal, with peaty streams tumbling down slopes clothed in pungent green bracken, rough yellowing grass, or wiry low-growing heather. For most of the way, their route followed a well-worn track which Cranstoun called a 'drove road', the path taken by farmers driving their beasts to market or to summer pastures.

"We are getting close to our destination," said Cranstoun a couple of hours later as they traversed a particularly boggy piece of ground. He pointed down the hill. "Round the next knoll and along the track for about a mile. 'Tis not far now."

But before they had travelled any further, Robert's attention was distracted by a low-growing plant under some bushes near a stream that trickled down the hill and across their path. *Tormentil.* An herbal remedy that would be a real boon for du Croc's malady. "Would you excuse me, my lords," he said, pulling his horse to the uphill side of the track. "I see some rare healing plants over there which I should collect. I can follow you down to the castle once my saddlebag is full."

Cranstoun and Ferniehirst shared a glance. "I will accompany you," said Sir Thomas, touching the hilt of his sword reflexively. "In case you miss the path."

"But…" Robert was about to protest that he would easily follow the tracks of such a large party, when he caught Sir Thomas and Michael exchanging another look. *There's something they're not saying. Mayhap they have highwaymen too.* "But that is too kind," he said, swinging down from his horse and pulling it out of the way of the rest of the group.

They waited until the queen and her attendants had all passed, then led their mounts over to a small tree and tied them up. Robert turned to Sir Thomas and gave him a questioning look.

"'Tis better not to travel these roads alone," was all the dark-haired lord replied.

Twenty minutes later, Robert had filled a bag with tormentil and was contemplating asking Sir Thomas if he had space in his pack to transport more, when, under a little clump of wizened trees some way upstream, he spotted a hint of purple that could be selfheal. "Let me just check up there," he called over to Ferniehirst, who stood guard with the horses.

But it was not healing herbs that Robert found under the rowans. As he approached, a low growl reached his ears, and he stopped, every nerve jangling and his hand flying to the dagger in his belt.

Do they have wolves in Scotland? Robert had not thought to ask, but he wished now that he'd brought a bow and arrow, for if he needed to use his sidearm, the wolf's fangs would likely be too close for comfort.

Back down the hill, Sir Thomas stood with the horses, and Robert silently beckoned him up the hill. Then, placing his pack carefully on the ground so both hands would be free, he pulled the blade from its sheath and crept forward to discover what kind of beast would make such a bloodcurdling noise.

~

Bothwell's ears pricked at the sound of hooves clattering down the track towards his castle. With a grimace, he pushed himself to his elbows. "Paris," he called to his manservant, "send a guard to fetch the English prisoners and bring them to the great hall. And find another two who can carry me down stairs." He threw back the covers, wincing at the pain in his side. "For I will not meet with the queen of Scots lying on my back in this dark tower."

Some minutes later, he sat on a padded chair, gulping spiced wine in an attempt to dull the pain, with his wife on one side and Paris on the other. *If I ever meet Jock Elliot again, he's a dead man,* Bothwell vowed. *He has made my life misery, and because of him I lost the prisoners I should have presented to the queen. If I lose my influence at court because of that...*

But he didn't get to finish that thought, for the studded oak doors at the entrance to the hall swung open, admitting the queen and her attendants.

"Help me up," he hissed, as the queen processed across the flagstone floor of his cavernous hall, her bearing regal and her expression kindly.

"My lord Bothwell," she greeted him, "I am so glad to see that the reports of your injuries 'ave been greatly exaggerated."

He inclined his head, the best approximation he could make to a bow whilst leaning on Paris' arm. "Your Grace, forgive me for the paucity of my welcome. My wounds recover, even if not as quickly as I would like. But I am happy to welcome you to my castle." He indicated the hewn-oak table pushed against the far wall, covered with platters and bowls overflowing with such delicacies as were available this far south in Scotland. "My servants have prepared luncheon. Perhaps you would like to eat? And then I have some prisoners for you."

Mary pursed her lips. "I think we should deal with the prisoners first. For we cannot tarry long—'tis a difficult journey, and 'twould be safer to return before dark."

Bothwell smiled grimly. *Perhaps this is my chance to recover some of my favour with the queen.* For his prisoners were English, caught in the very act of thieving a horse from the Armstrongs of Mangerton. After his fight with Little Jock, he might have lost the Scottish miscreants who'd languished in his dungeons, but surely two English reivers were worth more?

Jutting his chin, he motioned to a guard. "Bring in the prisoners!"

It was no wolf or other such carnivorous creature that met Robert. Instead, he found a wounded man lying at the foot of a rowan tree, his face grey, breath shallow and skin feverish. The jerkin and breeches the man wore above his grimy tunic were stained by a huge patch of blackened dried blood around his right hip and thigh, and when Robert investigated further, he discovered a bullet wound almost at the crease of his groin. Partly healed, it looked to be days old. *This man should be dead,* thought Robert. *And he will be soon, without some physic.* Perhaps even with it.

At that, Sir Thomas tiptoed around the tree, and caught his breath at the sight of Robert with the semi-conscious man. "Little Jock Elliot!" he exclaimed.

"Little?" questioned Robert, for his patient was a tall, lanky man who could hardly be called small. *Does my understanding of the English language fail me?*

"An ironic name," replied Ferniehirst. "Our Scots black humour at work." His eyes hardened. "But he's a notorious reiver and was responsible for wounding the earl of Bothwell, who the queen visits in his sickbed even as we speak." He drew his sword. "Stand back, and I will finish him off."

"No!" Robert leaned protectively over Elliot. "I am a doctor; bound by law to heal the sick and injured. Fetch my pack and I shall make a salve for his wound."

"You waste your time. He fought with the earl more than a week ago. This man is barely alive."

"Mayhap. But he has survived this long. He deserves a chance."

"Aye, a chance for the noose, more like," muttered Ferniehirst. But he turned on his heel and fetched Robert's saddlebag.

A few minutes later, Robert had mixed up a paste of calendula and applied it to the man's wound, and had built a fire to boil some water for a healing draught.

"You've applied your physic. What now?" asked Sir Thomas, leaning his shoulder against a nearby tree. "Little Jock is one of the Elliots of Park, who were on the lists for the queen's assizes. They escaped from Lord Bothwell, but this one will need to stand trial for his crimes—not to mention that he almost killed the earl. So you heal him, only for him to face the hangman. What is the point?"

"I'll tell ye the point," growled a voice in Robert's ear, as the point of a dirk dug viciously into his side. "Return me to my clan, if ye want to live to see the morn."

Robert's blood ran cold.

But with the realisation that his life was in danger came clarity of thought and a steely determination to overcome this miscreant. *After I tried to help him, this is all the thanks I get?* The gunshot wound would make Robert's adversary weak—and vulnerable, despite the weapon in his hand. Robert had the advantage of strength and fitness.

Tensing his muscles, Robert drove his elbow down into Jock's groin, aiming for the painful scar. It wasn't gentlemanly—but growing up on the streets of Paris had taught him how to survive. And you didn't survive for long if you played by the rules.

At the pain of the unexpected blow, Jock hunched forward, a hiss of pain escaping from between his teeth.

But Robert wasn't safe yet, and he followed his first blow with a sharp punch to the reiver's temple.

At this, the reiver toppled onto his side, the blade falling from his lifeless hand, eyes staring blankly, and lank, greasy hair flopping over his forehead.

Sir Thomas strode forward, sword in hand, and pushed at Jock's body with the toe of his boot. He raised an eyebrow. "I do believe you've done for him."

Taking the reiver's dagger in one hand, Robert felt for a pulse with the other. After a few moments, he looked up at Sir Thomas and nodded. "He's gone." Gently, he closed Jock's eyes. "God rest his soul."

Ferniehirst sheathed his sword. "For a doctor, you're a strange one. First you try to fix him, then you deliver a killing blow—and now you pray for his soul." He shook his head.

Robert shrugged. "Mais oui. As doctors, we try to heal, and not harm. But we have the right to expect the same from our patients—for if I am hurt, I cannot help anyone else." He got off his knees and stood up, brushing dirt off his britches. "In Paris, you learn to look after yourself. But you also learn that life is precious." He frowned down at Jock. "Even one such as this. He could have a wife and children depending on him." Robert sighed. "He should have thought of that before he tried to repay my kindness with the point of his knife. Help me load his body onto my horse and we can take him home for burial."

Sir Thomas put out a hand to stop Robert. "Nay, we can't do that. If we show up in Castleton carrying his body, we'll not get out alive. Let's take him to Hermitage and let Bothwell's soldiers take care of him."

Robert's first thought was to protest, but then he remembered what Libby had said of the reivers and their idea of justice, which took the biblical maxim of 'an eye for an eye' to its literal conclusion. Sir Thomas was right. Charity might be the ideal in God's eyes, but it was not the wise move here.

This borderland of Scotland truly is lawless. But there was something raw and primal here that attracted him; the rugged landscape, the valiant towns, the plain-speaking people—and a certain fair-haired lady with a shy smile. *I could grow to like it here.*

In contrast, Paris began to seem fanciful, busy and dirty. *But its people still need me.* They still needed his hospital. *I must remember my purpose here and not lose sight of my dreams.* Following his heart might be pleasant for a time, but it would not help the poor and dying of his birthplace. He needed to keep on track, using the opportunities that came his way when working for the ambassador to build his fortune and further his ambitions. *I must not fail.*

Nodding slowly, Robert let out a long breath. "Oui, you are right." He pointed at the horses. "Let us go to the castle."

CHAPTER 6

LIBBY's HEART WAS a-flutter all over again, for rather than the judgements the queen had expected, or the tête-à-tête Earl Bothwell might have wished for, there was to be a hand-fasting.

Michael Cranstoun of Stobs had spoken for one of the earl's English prisoners, Alexandra Graham, and now they were to be betrothed! 'Tis *so romantic*, thought Libby, as she stuck pins into the cramoisie and white silk dress Alexandra had borrowed from Bothwell's wife, Jean Gordon.

Half an hour later, Libby stood on her tiptoes to watch as Michael and Alexandra stood before the queen and exchanged their vows. And when the great hall of the castle erupted in cheering, she couldn't help herself; she sought the eyes of the Frenchman, who had sneaked into the back of the hall with Sir Thomas Ferniehirst just as the ceremony was starting.

The look he gave her in return made her cheeks burn and sent her heart racing once more. Somehow, with only the intensity of his gaze, he set a fire in her insides and emptied her mind. *I must... I must remember my purpose*, she thought, even as she memorised the sweep of his eyelashes, the strength of his brow, the golden flecks that made his brown eyes dance with light. *I need to find me a lord!* With an effort of will, she turned away, and went to congratulate Alexandra and Michael.

But, like iron attracted to a magnetic lode, when the queen's party set off northwards for Jedburgh again, Libby found herself riding alongside Robert, as if it was the only place she could be. She did not feel much like talking, however, so was happy to let the handsome Frenchman tell her about his work at the hospital in Paris; the eccentric characters he'd met and the strange ailments he'd healed.

Every now and again she'd sneak a glance at his profile, at the clean lines of his jaw and the way his brown hair fell over his forehead, at the tiny frown that creased his brow when he spoke with passion on subjects he cared about. He made being a doctor sound almost exciting. "Are there any women physicians where you work?" she started to ask, when she was interrupted by loud shouts and a rumpus from up near the head of their group.

At the sight that met her startled gaze, Libby's chest clenched with fear.

Ahead of them, Mary's white palfrey had slipped on the muddy path, and sent the queen careening down a bank and into a foul-smelling bog. Almost instantly, Mary began to sink into the loathsome mire, but, just as quickly, the Englishwoman, Alexandra Graham, had leapt off her horse and was stretched out on the mud trying to reach the queen.

Stuck on the narrow path near the back of the group, Libby and Robert, along with most of the queen's party, could only watch with horror as their monarch was sucked deeper and deeper into the mud. Mary had sunk almost to her armpits before Alexandra, aided by Laird Cranstoun and Sir Thomas Ferniehirst, was able to pull her out of the bog.

Covered in mud from the top of her head to tip of her calfskin boots, and shivering violently, the queen appeared shocked but unharmed.

"Thank the Lord!" exclaimed Libby.

Leaping off his horse, Robert handed Libby the reins. "Hold him for me. I should go check on Her Grace."

By the time Robert reached the queen and her rescuers where they huddled on the rough grass at the edge of the bog, Sir Thomas had exhibited presence of mind by offering Mary his cloak, and then hurried off to find more dry cloaks for Alexandra and Michael from amongst the other lords.

"Your Grace," Robert stopped before the queen and quickly inclined his head. "Are you injured? Do you need medical attention?"

Mary shook her head. "I don't think so." But her whole body trembled, and her skin—

as much as he could see of it under the mud—was even paler than usual.

'tis probably just the cold—and the shock. But she needs dry clothes, as soon as possible, or she could catch a chill. "Do you have a spare dress you could wear?" Robert asked, as Maitland and Flam joined the group around the queen.

"Not 'ere." Tendrils of muddy hair stuck to the queen's cheeks as she shook her head.

"Try to keep warm then. And please call on me if you feel sick or light-headed."

"We need to get you moving, ma'am," Flam interrupted, pulling Ferniehirst's cloak tighter around the queen's shoulders, "and into some dry clothes."

Exactly what I just said. Robert took a step backwards, wondering at this change of attitude from the queen's lady-in-waiting. *Did I offend her?*

But he got his answer a moment later when Libby joined them. "The earl of Huntly holds our horses," she whispered to him, leaning so close it almost took his breath away.

The look that Flam gave them could have curdled milk. *She is jealous.* That would explain her rudeness a moment ago.

"How is the queen?" continued Libby, oblivious to Flam's cool demeanour.

"Unharmed. But we need to keep her dry and warm." Robert sought out Laird Cranstoun, their party leader, and touched his arm. "Sire, would we be able to intrude on your hospitality once more? The queen needs to get into dry clothes as soon as possible."

"Of course." Cranstoun looked northwards. "We should ride for Stobs with all haste. I will send word to get hot baths prepared—and fresh clothes."

It took several pails of fresh hot water and the ministrations of Flam, Libby and Cranstoun's housekeeper, before Mary was finally warm—and clean—enough to dress in the borrowed, but blessedly dry, clothes provided for her at Stobs. Sitting in a heavy oak chair with a blanket wrapped around her and a posset of wine and milk clutched in her hand, she finally stopped shivering.

Her own physician having cried off from the long journey, Libby insisted that Mary allow the ambassador's French physician to examine her before they resumed their journey. "You suffered a heavy fall, ma'am. You may carry an injury without realising."

And so it was that the handsome Frenchman—who, she had noticed, could not take his eyes off Lady Preston—held her wrist with his fingers for almost a full minute before putting the back of his hand against her forehead. With a satisfied nod, he declared that she appeared not to have contracted a chill, or at least not yet, and that her heart was strong.

'Tis a wonder after all that my husband has put me through. For Darnley was feckless and wanton, known to frequent the taverns and whore-houses of Edinburgh, and constantly badgering Mary to give him the crown matrimonial.

Mary might have considered this, had he shown more interest in the minutiae of government—but he was so uninterested in the day-to-day proceedings of state that she had to get a stamp made of his signature, since he was so seldom around to sign official documents. He preferred hunting and hawking.

But in Darnley's arrogance he wanted to be *more* than just a co-ruler. There were whispers that he intended to take the throne from her by force. Fortunately, he had few supporters, as he had alienated most of the nobles as well as his wife. So, whilst he might scheme and plot, thus far her informants had not heard of any firm plans. But Mary expected to hear from the French king, Charles the ninth, any day now, with the latest from his spies.

A polite cough told her that the Frenchman wasn't finished with her. "I must check for internal injuries. May I?" he asked, before carefully palpating her stomach with the flat of his hand.

As his investigations reached her right side, she winced.

"That hurts?"

"Only my old trouble. My spleen. Lusgerie gives me a draught from time to time. I must need me another."

"You are sure 'tis not new?"

She shook her head, and Monsieur Nau straightened.

"You should rest, ma'am, and recover from this ordeal. You are young and strong, but 'tis not long since you were with child. I am sure Laird Cranstoun would give you a bed here for the night."

Mary waved her hand at him dismissively. "If my strength will serve me, I can find it in my heart to do anything. And I need to return to Jedburgh this night." *If Charles' letter has arrived, I will need to reply.* She pressed her lips together. *And I may need to take action.*

CHAPTER 7

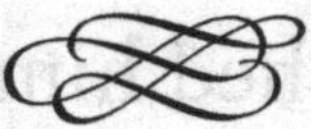

THURSDAY 17TH OCTOBER 1566

THE NEXT MORNING, Robert allowed himself to skip his usual run. Riding fifty miles the previous day had left his body stiff and aching. *I will ask the innkeep for a hot bath tonight. That should help.*

But, despite the long day, the drama of the queen's accident, and their late return to Jedburgh, Robert was not tired and his spirits were high. He spent the morning working with the herbs he'd collected—cleaning, chopping, and preparing salves and infusions. Whilst he worked, memories from the previous day filled his mind—the curve of a cheek, the ghost of a smile, the twinkle of an eye.

She had bewitched him, this Scottish lass, with her quiet ways and beguiling looks. For a time, he allowed himself to daydream of taking her back to France, introducing her to his brother, showing her his work at the hospital… Then his hands stilled, and he stared out of the window for a long while. *It cannot be.* A lady like this would never associate herself with one such as him, nor show interest in work as menial as that of the sickroom. He had to remember that and not let his heart be captured by a love that was beyond his reach.

With a sigh, he began to tidy away his tools and potions. *I will have to avoid her. That is the only way. And then I might meet another maid and disremember this fair lass.*

Robert's efforts to forget her would be

helped if the ambassador didn't require his attendance when he next met with the Scottish queen. *I shall hope for that.* If need be, Robert could feign sickness. And then in a few days they would return to Edinburgh, and he could put this matter behind him as a mere pleasant memory of his time in Jedburgh. *Oui. That is the way. She will be just a pleasant memory.* Nothing more.

Libby sat at the rough wooden table in the barrel-vaulted kitchen of the tower house and stared groggily into her bowl of porridge. To her left, the queen's red-faced cook conferred with the earl of Moray, who had come downstairs on some errand or other.

Awakened rudely this morning by a hammering on the front door, Libby's first thought was that they were being attacked, and a flashback to the attack on Preston Tower had paralyzed her with fear. Even after reassurances by Alexandra—who'd been sharing her tiny room—it had taken some minutes for her heart to return from her mouth to its usual position in her chest.

By the time she and the Englishwoman were dressed, Libby's nerves were less of a jangle. Even so, her hands shook as she tied the last ribbons and buttons, and every third or fourth breath she had to suck in a deep draught or she was sure she would suffocate.

With Alexandra summoned to meet with her father and the queen in the great hall, Libby was left alone in the garret. From past experience, she knew that the only way she'd be able to leave the bedroom this morning would be to assuage her worries by taking control.

The small room did not take much to put right—but it did not take much to make it disorderly either. The pallet Alexandra had been using needed tidying as did the covers on Libby's bed. And the hairbrush and jewellery box on the windowsill were misaligned, and her shoes tucked at the end of the bed were not properly straight. Once she'd fixed those, Libby opened her trunk and removed all the contents so she could re-stack her dresses and undergarments.

Only when everything in the room was finally tidy and ordered did Libby's anxieties calm and her breathing become more regular. She sat for a moment on her bed until she was sure her body would not let her down, then took a deep breath, opened the door and crept down the stone stairs.

Despite Alexandra's reassurances, Libby checked at every window to ensure that there were no soldiers in the orchard, or reivers in the street. But all was quiet, and she finally began to believe that they were safe.

It was only then that her thoughts turned

to the events of the previous day. It had started out so well, with the Frenchman's entertaining company on the ride to Stobs, and Alexandra's betrothal to Laird Cranstoun. But then the queen had nearly died in that foul bog, and the rest of the day had passed in a blur.

And so she sat at breakfast in a fog of memories, distractedly supping gruel and drinking goat's milk.

"Get that porridge finished, lass, and get out of my hair!" Cook brought Libby rudely back to the present as she bustled past with a steaming platter which she handed to the earl. "Now the queen has her breakfast, I need to get everything packed and ready for transport to Hume."

Briefly, Libby wondered why Moray fetched the queen's porridge himself, rather than sending a servant. *He must meet with her this morning. That will be it.*

But Libby's thoughts quickly turned to

the upcoming trip, for today they were to ride for her step-father's castle near Kelso, on the next stage of Mary's progress through the Borders. *I must pack! I must get ready to ride...* Libby's hand flew to her mouth. *The queen's dress!* Mary's riding outfit had been ruined yesterday when she fell in the mire. *Before I do anything else, I need to see if it can be fixed. Mayhap we can wash it or sponge the soiled parts.* But that would not be an easy task, judging from the way the queen had looked when she was pulled from the bog. She had been covered from head to toe in thick black mud and looked very sorry for herself.

Libby pushed the plate away and stood up. *This will be a challenge.* But she loved working with the queen's clothes, so it would be a challenge she'd enjoy.

Slowly ascending the stairs to her small chamber in the tower house with Flam Fleming accompanying her, conflicting emotions buoyed Mary's spirits and yet caused her shoulders to droop and her steps to drag. She felt great satisfaction that she had managed to mediate between Alexandra and her father and that the English heiress was to wed Laird Cranstoun—or rather, *Sir* Michael Cranstoun, as Mary had dubbed him after he rescued her from the mire. There would be a happy ending to that story, she was sure.

However, she was less happy about how her body fared this morning. Attended by Lord Graham and the others in the great hall of the tower house, she had put on a brave face, wanting to appear regal in front of the English lord. She dared not appear otherwise, lest word get back to her cousin Elizabeth that the Scottish queen was weak or unfit.

But weak and unfit was exactly how she felt. Every bone in her body ached, her chest was cramped and her insides seemed to contain a great stone. 'Twas *a wonder I could eat breakfast this morning.* But now she was decidedly queasy, and the very idea of food turned her stomach.

Flam followed the queen into her small room. "Ma'am, forgive me, but you don't look well. Should I fetch Doctor Lusgerie?"

Mary had learned from her mother that there were times when a monarch needed to be strong and independent, and that there were times when they should graciously accept help from others. This was one of those times. "Please. I think my old trouble returns."

~

"Just a chill," Lusgerie pronounced after he examined the queen, and the good news quickly travelled from Flam to the other Maries and Libby, who had resorted to soaking the queen's velvet dress in a barrel of water. It might ruin the nap, but the mud was too deeply ingrained to sponge off, so she'd been left with no other choice.

Libby *could* have passed the task off to a servant, but since she had volunteered to organise the queen's wardrobe, she felt it her duty to at least *try* to redeem the ruined riding outfit. However, the longer she spent on it, the more she became convinced that the dress was beyond repair. Even if the velvet could be returned to its previous lustre and cleanliness, the lace trim looked grubby and grey, and the whole outfit had lost its body, hanging limply like a flag at half-mast.

Before she gave up completely, Libby decided to leave the dress overnight to dry, in the faint hope that it might somehow improve if she just left it for twenty-four hours.

Some minutes later, she was back in the main hall with the rest of the ladies. At the wide stone fireplace they gathered around, the talk was of the queen's condition, which seemed to have worsened.

"She complains of her old illness," Ebba Seton said as she pricked a needle into the large tapestry of Jacob and Esau the ladies were working on. "But Lusgerie maintains 'tis merely a chill, from falling in the bog."

Flam raised her eyebrows. "If 'tis merely a chill, then why does her side hurt so? And why does she vomit? Libby," Flam speared Libby with her dark eyes, "what would your young doctor say? What would be *his* diagnosis?"

"M—my doctor?" Libby stuttered. "I'm sure I don't know what you mean."

"The young Frenchman you rode with

the other day." With a tilt of her chin, Flam added, "He hardly left your side."

For a moment, Libby was lost for words. *Is everyone talking about me?* Gossip like that could ruin her chances of a match with a rich lord. *I must deflect her questions. And I must never see Robert again. I cannot have people speculating about me and one such as him, however handsome he might be.*

Flicking a hand dismissively, Libby tried to affect an air of unconcern. "Oh, I was using him to gather information about the fashions in Paris for the next gown I'll make. I have no idea about his doctoring."

Flam raised an eyebrow, but let it go. "Well, if 'tis her spleen, we shall be here some days yet." She smoothed the section of canvas she was working on. "Mayhap we might even get this finished afore we go."

CHAPTER 8

FRIDAY 18TH OCTOBER, 1566

BOTHWELL CRUMPLED THE letter in his hand. *Damn this injury! And may Jock Elliot be damned to hell!* It was nearly two weeks since he had been wounded, and still he was unable to walk more than a step or two before the pain crippled him.

But, despite their agreement during the queen's visit a couple of days ago, it seemed she now planned to ride north rather than waiting until he was well enough to bring the Armstrongs and Elliots to her. *And I am too sick to ride to her and set her right.* With a curse, he slammed his fist into the feather mattress he lay upon.

A man of action more than words, this inactivity was killing him. And being stuck down here at Hermitage when Moray and Maitland had the ear of the queen up in Jedburgh caused bile to rise in his throat every time he thought of it.

If it hadn't been for Jock Elliot, playing dead and then attacking the earl and almost killing him, the Armstrongs would never have escaped. And, if not for his injury, Bothwell would have been in Jedburgh with the queen these last days, presiding over her assizes and, as Lieutenant of the Borders, giving her advice. More importantly, his presence would have sidelined James Stewart, Earl of Moray.

Moray might be Mary's bastard half-brother, but he was a slippery fish with designs on her throne—or the regency at the very least. Every last piece of trouble Mary had encountered in her reign so far—castigation by that Protestant firebrand, John Knox; open rebellion from the lords of the congregation; and, most recently, the murder of her private secretary, David Riccio—you could be sure that Moray had a hand in it. He was a master at pulling strings, lighting fires and whispering sedition—and also at disappearing into the woodwork like the worm he was, as soon as anyone came looking for someone to blame.

There weren't many men that Bothwell liked, but Moray was one he hated more than most. And yet, serving Mary Stuart at court meant he had to paste a false smile onto his face and deal with the slimy bastard so often it made his skin crawl. *I need to be rid of that man. He will always stand in my way, no matter what I do or say.* And Bothwell had ambitions that stretched *far* beyond this castle and the rolling countryside of the

Borders. But if Moray knew of Bothwell's plans, he would do all in his power to thwart them. *I need to keep one step ahead of the bastard.*

"Paris," Bothwell beckoned his mouse-like page, "I need you to go to Jedburgh and bring back news for me. See what the people whisper of the privy council, and of the queen. And most especially of the earl of Moray." He handed the man a few coins. "Leave now, so I may get word as soon as possible!"

~

Libby's pessimism about Mary's ruined dress was unfortunately well-founded. Next day when she went to check it, she found it had dried well but also shrunk a little, so that the lace creased and puckered where it was attached to the seams. And because the queen was of above-average height, the whole outfit would now be too short for her. Libby sighed. 'Tis *irreparable.*

I'll have to tell her. But I'll offer to make her a new dress. If we order fabric today and I work every spare minute, I should have it ready in time for her trip. I'll work all night if need be. However, before Libby could do that, she'd need to tell the queen, and get authorisation to order more material from the Edinburgh cloth merchant the royal household favoured.

Rapping lightly on the door of the queen's bedchamber, Libby licked her lips, mentally rehearsing what she would say to Mary as an apology for not being able to redeem her outfit.

When there was no reply, she knocked again, and then cautiously pushed the door open.

Drapes covered the windows, but through the gloom Libby could make out the queen's prone figure on the bed. *She is sleep-*

ing. But something in Mary's pose struck Libby as odd, and she crept closer. The queen's breathing was shallow and laboured, and a gloss of sweat sheened her forehead.

With a frown, Libby touched the back of her hand to the queen's cheek. *She is burning up!* Libby's mouth went dry. "Wake up, ma'am," she said, giving Mary's arm a little shake.

When that elicited no response, Libby spoke louder, and shook Mary's shoulder harder—but to no avail. Whatever she did, the queen was unresponsive, just lying on her bed with an unhealthy pallor to her skin and damp tendrils of auburn hair sticking to her brow.

Her feet hardly touching the stone treads, Libby flew down the stairs to the great hall and grabbed a page by the arm. "Go fetch Doctor Lusgerie." At the boy's puzzled expression, she added, "Now!"

"What's wrong?" Mary Seton jumped up

from her sewing, her face aghast, and hurried over to where Libby stood by the door.

"The queen," Libby replied, her stomach churning. "I can't wake her."

Flam put down her needlework. "What did I say? Lusgerie was mistaken when he said it was just a chill."

Libby lifted a shoulder. "Mayhap. But we need him now. She is running a fever and I could not rouse her."

By this time Ebba Seton had rushed from the room, and Libby followed her up the stairs. Tying back the drapes so they could see what they were doing, Libby asked, "Should we try to cool her?"

"'Twould be better to be guided by Lusgerie," Ebba replied. "But where is Beth? It was her turn to sit with the queen. She should've seen how ill Mary is and called the doctor."

"Perhaps she has already gone to fetch

him?" Libby suggested, as Flam and Mary Livingston joined them in the turret room.

The corner of Ebba's mouth turned down. "Or perhaps she has slipped out to meet that husband of hers. She would surely have stopped to tell us if the queen's condition had worsened."

In the moment's silence that followed, nobody jumped to Beth Beaton's defence. Then Flam pushed past the others and took the queen's hand, sitting on the narrow bed opposite the queen's. It was the bed that she had occupied every night since an intruder had been found under Mary's bed at Rossend Castle.

This sleeping arrangement meant that Flam had to be more creative if she wished a liaison with a handsome gentleman, but it protected the queen's reputation any time her husband, Lord Darnley, did not share her bedchamber. And, if rumours were to be believed, that had been the case almost every night since Mary had fallen pregnant with the young Prince James, for Darnley was not in favour.

Flam lifted Mary's fingers to her lips and kissed them. "Your Grace," she crooned, "wake up!"

They were still grouped worriedly around the unconscious queen ten minutes later when Doctor Lusgerie finally arrived. Quickly assessing the situation, he sent Libby for a bowl of cold water and some clean cloths, asked Ebba to bring a bowl of hot water and a drying flannel, and sent the other Maries away 'to give him room to work'.

On their way to the kitchen to fetch the supplies, Libby and Ebba bumped into Livvy Livingston on the stairs.

"Where were you?" demanded Ebba. "The queen is sick!"

Livvy's face blanched. "But... I only left

her for a minute. I went into the garden for some air."

Ebba narrowed her eyes. "It's been at least ten minutes since Libby found the queen unconscious. If anything happens to her, you will have to live with that."

CHAPTER 9

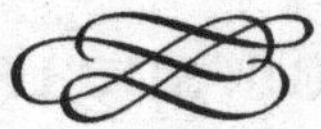

SATURDAY 19TH OCTOBER 1566

"UNCONSCIOUS, THEY SAY," said du Croc from his seat in a large wooden chair beside the fire in their room at the Carter's Rest. "'Tis a chill. She fell sick after a riding accident." He crossed a fat ankle over his knee, and rubbed gingerly at his foot, wrinkling his white hose.

"When she fell in the bog?" asked Robert, his stomach sinking.

"Oui."

I should have insisted she rested at Stobs. Obviously the queen's constitution is not as strong as she thinks. "Do they give her elderflower and ginger?"

The ambassador speared Robert with a sharp look. "I know nothing of her treatment. She has her own physician. I am sure she has more than adequate care."

With a small nod, Robert turned to lean on the oak mantelpiece, staring into the fire. *Lusgerie will no doubt bleed the queen, maybe even purge her.* His jaw clenched involuntarily. *The man's ideas are outdated.* Lusgerie could end up making Mary *more* unwell, rather than healing her. *But I can say nothing. She is not my patient.*

Du Croc beckoned McMann over from where he sat at a desk by the window. "Édouard, I need to write to tell the king of the Scots queen's illness. Fetch your quill."

Lusgerie bled the queen, but the only other treatment he recommended was to reduce her temperature with cold compresses.

So Libby, Ebba, Beth and Flam agreed a rota to sit with the queen and keep her cool, ready to alert Lusgerie at any time if her condition worsened. But Ebba would not trust Mary Livingston to sit alone with the queen; instead she made Livvy accompany the others during the long hours of darkness when they could read to each other to help stay awake.

Libby had the first watch that afternoon, and as she pressed a damp pad to the queen's forehead, the enormity of the situation hit her properly. This was the queen of Scotland, lying unconscious in an un-prepossessing house in an ordinary town, with only Libby to watch over her, and nothing to heal her save some cold water.

Is there no herbal draught we could give her? Or flowers we can spread whose aroma will keep the evil spirits away?

Libby could not understand why Lusgerie would not try more, try *harder*, for the queen. *I'm sure Robert would have tried some other cure, rather than just leaving the queen senseless.* Libby felt traitorous for the thought, but it niggled at her even as she straightened the queen's bedclothes and tidied her auburn hair. Libby had vowed not to see Robert again, but… If Mary's life was at stake, surely she should try everything?

Her restlessness took her to the window, where she pulled back the drape and looked out over the garden to the slow-moving Jed Water beyond. *Robert is younger, so he will not be as experienced a physician as Lusgerie. Mayhap Lusgerie is right. But Robert qualified as a doctor much more recently than Lusgerie, so will know all the newer cures.* She chewed her lip. Could it do any harm to ask? Surely a few herbs would not make the queen worse? And they might even improve her condition. *I will go and find him,* she decided, *after Ebba relieves me.*

CHAPTER 10

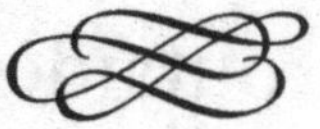

ROBERT HAD JUST sat down for dinner in the crowded salon of the Carter's Rest when the landlady bustled over and touched him on the arm.

"Beggin' yer pardon, sire." With a chapped hand twitching at the seam of her worsted skirts, she bobbed a coarse attempt at a curtsey. "There's a young lady to see ye. I tried to make her, but she wouldnae come in."

A young lady. Robert's heart leaped. Could

it be Libby? Wiping his mouth with a napkin, he hurried out, forgetting all his fine resolutions to avoid consorting with the Scottish lass.

He found her outside, standing on the hard-packed dirt of Abbey Place, woollen cloak drawn tightly around her shoulders against the chill of evening. In the wan light spilling from the leaded windows of the inn, Libby's face looked grey and drawn.

"My lady! Are you well?"

"Aye, I'm fine." Libby chewed her lip, and glanced up at him, blue eyes dark with misgiving. "'Tis the queen."

"Oui. I heard she was sick."

Libby nodded. "Lusgerie has bled her, but still she lies unconscious. I—" Taking a deep breath, she looked down at her hands, knotted together in front of her kirtle. "I wondered if there was anything else we could do? Some herbs, a salve..." She grimaced. "Lusgerie has us sponging her with cold water. But it seems too little." Looking up at him again, lines of worry etched her forehead. "She is the *queen*. Surely we can do more?"

Robert wanted to take her hands in his, to smooth away the frown from her brow and reassure her that the queen would recover. But he could not do that. It would not be right. Or truthful. "What are her symptoms?"

"She has a fever—she sweats, and her breathing is shallow. And she hasn't woken since yesterday. When she was last awake, she complained of her old trouble—her spleen—and it made her vomit."

Robert sucked a breath through his teeth. *This is not good.* "Could I examine her?"

Libby's hands balled into fists. "'Twould not be right. Lusgerie is her physician. He'd be offended if he even knew I was speaking to you."

"But still you came," Robert replied softly,

and this time he *did* take her hands in his. *Propriety be damned.*

Her breath caught. "Ah—Aye. You qualified more recently than Lusgerie. I thought you—" she looked down at their linked hands, "—I thought you might know some cure that he had not heard of."

"You could've sent a messenger," he said, a smile tickling his lips.

She glanced up at him again. "But word might've got back to Lusgerie. This way, I can take your cure back to her and treat her when it's my turn to watch over her."

He lifted her fingers to his lips and kissed her hand. "I am gratified by your faith in me, my lady." Nodding in the direction of the inn's upper floor, he added, "But all my supplies are in our rooms. Will you wait here, or accompany me upstairs?"

Libby's gaze darted up and down the street, then at the darkened upper floor of the inn. She seemed undecided.

"I can ask McMann to join us."

She shook her head. "No. 'Twill be fine."

With a curt nod, Robert tucked one of her hands into his elbow, and escorted her into the inn.

~

Du Croc's parlour was bigger than Libby had expected, with a window overlooking the street, a large fireplace in the side wall, and doors on either side which presumably led to their bedchambers.

Robert indicated for Libby to wait by the door while he lit some candles. Then he motioned her to a well-polished oak chair. "Sit by the fire while I gather some things for you."

Libby watched, fascinated, as he delved into a specially made case containing row upon row of small wooden drawers, each with a carefully scribed label slotted in the front, and filled with all manner of dried flowers, leaves and roots. After a few minutes, he called her over.

"Right," he said, smoothing out a large piece of paper and scooping some herbs into the centre. "Add a spoonful of this mint to boiling water and then let it cool. Then soak the cloths you use to soothe the queen's fever in the mixture." Twisting the corners of the paper together, he made them into a small parcel and handed it to her.

Libby tucked the package into the pocket of her cloak.

Next, he gave her a mixture of ginger and elderflower. "If you can get her to drink, then make her a tea with these herbs. They will help reduce the pain in her spleen."

"I will try."

Finally, he gave her a small pottery container with a strong-smelling paste inside. "Spread this on her chest," he rubbed the area above his breastbone to show her where he meant, "three times a day until she awakens. The aroma will fill her senses and it should be enough to reach through her swoon and rouse her."

Libby nodded. "I hope so." She took the pot and looked up at him. In the candlelight, his dark eyes were fathomless, like a deep well that she could drown in, were she not careful. *Why does he have to be so handsome?* If he were plain, like Hugh Somerville, it would be easier. But standing this close to him, surrounded by the scent of sandalwood that she was starting to associate with him, her heart pounded in her ears and she found it hard to breathe. He was intoxicating. So intoxicating, that earlier, when he had kissed her hand, she had thought she might faint.

With a huge effort of will, she broke from his gaze and stuffed the pot in her pocket. "Thank you, sire, I am most grateful."

Donning his cloak and hat, he offered her

his arm again, "Come. I will accompany you back to Hartrigge House."

~

At the news that Paris brought back from Jedburgh, Bothwell almost howled in dismay. It seemed that the queen had taken ill as a result of her trip to visit him and lay near death in her lodgings.

"But her physician attends, sire." Paris twirled his hat nervously. "Lusgerie, the old Frenchman. He has bled her."

"Pah! That leech will be the death of her! All he wants is to drink her brandy and take her coin. And when he's saved enough gold that he need no longer work, he'll drink himself into oblivion!" Bothwell motioned his servant closer. "Help me up, Paris. I need to get to Jedburgh."

But it was no use. Bothwell hadn't even reached the door of his room when his legs gave way and, if it hadn't been for his servant's arm under his shoulders, he would've ended up in a sorry heap on the cold stone floor of his bedchamber.

Sat on the edge of his bed a minute later, Bothwell growled in frustration. "How am I to help the queen when I cannot even walk three steps unaided?"

Paris cleared his throat. "Mayhap we could carry you, sire?"

"All the way to Jedburgh?" Bothwell scoffed. "There are not enough men in my garrison." But the man's suggestion gave him an idea. "But... Go to the captain of my guard. Tell him to fashion a horse litter and make ready to leave as soon as possible!"

IT DIDN't TAKE long for them to walk the short distance to the tower house, but it allowed Libby a few minutes to quiz Robert on his knowledge of herbs.

"Monsieur Paré, who I worked under at l'hôpital, believed greatly in the power of nature to heal and rehabilitate," he explained. "Much of the work we did there—especially with the poor, who could not afford expensive drugs—was to test cures from folklore, from the village healers of history." He lifted a shoulder. "And many of them worked."

Libby frowned. "But—forgive me for asking—did people not think you charlatans? Surely they would expect more than a few herbs?"

Robert shrugged again. "When you have nothing, then something given freely, even a few herbs, is cause for gratitude. And we did not give them *just* herbs—remember, there was science involved. We dispensed draughts, salves, medicines... I even discovered a way to mix ground herbs with oil and flour to make a type of biscuit which could be cut into pieces and swallowed in a daily dose. And anyway," he stopped at the corner of Canongate and gave her a teasing look, "if you think me a charlatan, why then did you come asking for my help?"

Her mouth in a line, Libby searched his face. *Will it do any harm to tell him?* She could surely give him some of the facts without revealing the whole truth? "When I was unwell some time ago, an old woman from our village healed me with some herbs." She lifted a shoulder. "So, when the queen was ill I thought it worth a try." Catching his eye, she added, "I know that you stopped to collect herbs on our way to Hermitage."

His eyebrow quirked. "Word travels fast."

"There is not much that escapes court gossip."

A flash of concern crossed his face. "Then we should not tarry here, lest people misconstrue our purpose." Resuming their route towards the queen's house, Robert questioned her further. "In your village—what is it called?"

"Preston."

"In Preston, is there no physician, that you needed an herbal healer?"

Libby did not reply immediately. *How can I explain, without revealing too much?* "He—is not very sympathetic. With women's problems." That would surely be enough to convince Robert, without provoking further investigation.

But, unlike most men she had encountered, Robert was not deterred by her mention of feminine issues. "You have problems with your monthly flow? Oil of evening primrose can help." His brows knit together. "Do you have that here in Scotland?"

Libby waved a hand at him, colour rising in her cheeks.

Robert gasped. "Humble apologies, my lady. I have embarrassed you." His shoulders drooped. "In my enthusiasm to help and to heal, I forget that not everyone likes to talk of such matters."

The clump of heavy footsteps behind them saved Libby from replying.

"My lady Preston, is that you?" Puffing loudly, Hugh Somerville caught them up, then doffed his hat in her direction.

"Good evening Master Somerville." Libby bobbed a small curtsey.

"I've not met your companion." Hugh tilted his head at the Frenchman.

Robert squeezed her elbow warningly and jumped in with a reply. "Robert Nau at your service, sire." Taking off his velvet bonnet, he gave a quick bow. "I work for Philibert du Croc, the French ambassador. Lady Preston has been giving me an update on the queen's condition."

Libby gave him a sideways glance. *He was careful not to mention his actual position with the ambassador. Clever.*

"Ah. Yes." Hugh wiped his face with a linen kerchief, then addressed Libby. "How is Her Grace?"

What can I tell him? Libby was unsure what rumours circulated the town. Was it better to be honest, or to allay worries? *Probably the latter.* "She is still ill. But she's under Doctor Lusgerie's care. I'm sure she will be back to full health soon."

Hugh seemed satisfied with this explanation. "Good, good. Now," he stuffed the kerchief into a pocket in his trunk hose. "I came to see if you were free to take a turn around the town again? If your business with the ambassador is finished?"

Robert released her arm and gave a small bow. "Quite finished, sire."

"But—" Libby's hand fluttered to her mouth.

"My lady, I shall keep you no longer. Enjoy your walk." With a nod, Robert turned on his heel and strode off in the direction of the Carter's Rest.

Libby stared after him, wondering if it was just a trick of the light, or if that had been a look of anguish that crossed his face before he left. Why would he be so upset? Was it because Hugh had interrupted them? *Or mayhap because he had to misdirect Hugh as to my purpose this evening?* That would be it. Robert seemed an honest man, and it would pain him to tell a falsehood, she was sure.

Stiffening her spine, she addressed Somerville. "My lord, I am afraid I cannot walk with you. I need to return to the tower house. 'Tis my turn to sit with the queen." She hoped God would forgive her for the small falsehood, for the last thing she wanted right now was Hugh's company. Compared to the Frenchman, he seemed boorish and dull—and, regardless, she needed to get Robert's cures to the queen.

But Hugh is a lord, she reminded herself, and gave him a weak smile. "Mayhap tomorrow the queen will be recovered and we ladies will be free to explore the town again."

His long legs carrying him quickly up Canongate, the wide street that ran from the river to the marketplace, Robert silently cursed himself for his ill-mannered words. *What will Libby think of me? To discuss*

such delicate matters with a noblewoman is unthinkable. I treated her as if she were one of my medical colleagues, not a refined lady!

It would serve him right if she never wanted to speak to him again. His heart twisted at the thought, and his spirits plummeted. Despite his resolution the other day, he could not forget her—did not *want* to forget her.

But I should. For it seems she has a suitor. By his dress and manners, this Somerville was some rich Scottish lord with designs on Libby, even if he spoke more slowly than an archbishop at a funeral mass and had a face that resembled a flaxen-haired longhorn cow. *But even an ugly lord is far more suited to a fine lady than one such as I.*

For Robert had nothing to offer Libby— save a few herbal remedies. No land, no title, no fortune or large chateau in the countryside. Just his friendship, his conversation... and his heart.

Robert shook his head in despair. Seeing her again this evening had rekindled his feelings and set a fire in his belly that logic and reason could not douse. He felt empty without her. Was this love? Or just enchantment?

In France, he had come across his fair share of beautiful women, and been attracted to many of them. He had drawn the attention of courtesans and learned the ways of amour. But his heart had never been captivated like this before. He had never lost sleep, nor woken from fevered dreams of any of the mademoiselles of Paris.

At the very least, this is infatuation, he thought, as he pushed open the door of the Carter's Rest and made his way to the salon. He set his jaw. If it was a mere infatuation, then he would get over it, in time. He just needed to remember his earlier resolution and try to avoid her. *Without kindling there is no flame.* And without

Libby, there would be no dolour. No colour or warmth either, but at least no heartache.

"A flagon of ale!" he called to the landlady, sitting himself on a rough wooden bench beside the worthy McMann. Perhaps the beer would dampen his feelings. It was worth a try.

Back at Hartrigge House, Libby's first stop was the kitchen on the ground floor. It was a large space, but when filled with bustling servants and the rotund, white-clad cook, it seemed crowded.

Libby helped herself to a couple of crockery pots from a shelf of cookware, then crossed over to the fire and ladled boiling water into each one. Into the first she shook some of the soothing mint, which she would leave in her room overnight until it cooled.

To the other, she added a little of the ginger and elderflower.

But before she escaped the kitchen, cook's heavy hand landed on her shoulder. "What's that you got, lass?"

To her chagrin, Libby jumped, embarrassing herself further by squeaking with fright. Clearing her throat in an effort to disguise her discomfiture, she drew herself to her full height and stared down at the dumpy woman. "A draught for the queen, from the doctor.""Tis *not a lie*, she thought. *I just neglected to mention which doctor.*

For a moment, Cook narrowed her eyes at Libby as if about to say something. But then she gave a little shake of her head, making her ginger curls rattle around her face like seeds on a sycamore. She flapped a hand. "Be gone with ye, then, lass. Some of us hae work to do down here."

Libby scuttled out of the kitchen, clutching the two pots to her chest as she climbed the turnpike stair. *My next hurdle is Ebba Seton.* But first she should stow the mint infusion in her room and remove her cloak.

Once that was done, Libby hurried down the stairs again, and stopped on the stone landing outside the queen's room. A heavy drape hung on the wall, covering the small turret window and guarding against the chill of the October evening.

Carefully, Libby tucked the herbal tea out of sight on the windowsill behind the thick fabric. Then she quietly pushed open the door and tiptoed into the queen's room.

At her entrance, Ebba looked up questioningly. "'Tis not time yet for your shift?"

Libby shrugged. "No—but I thought I would relieve you so you could go eat dinner."

Ebba looked unconvinced. "I'm not—"

"There's wild boar." Libby licked her lips. "And honeyed pears with almonds."

The older woman set down her needlework and lifted her chin. "Honeyed pears, you say?"

"Yes. Monk's Pear from the orchard. 'Twas very sweet."

Ebba stood. "Well, if you're sure." She stepped to the door. "Thank you. I'll not stay away long."

As soon as Ebba left, Libby set to work.

Rubbing her palms together to warm her hands, she whispered an apology to the unconscious woman, then undid the ribbons at the top of the queen's chemise. Next, Libby dabbed some of the salve from the pot Robert had given her onto the paper-white skin of Mary's chest, spreading the greasy mixture thinly, as the physician had directed. It had a pungent smell which made her eyes water, and very quickly the sharp aroma filled the room.

After re-tying the queen's linen shift, Libby returned to the hallway and retrieved the ginger and elderflower tea. Then she put an arm under the queen's shoulders, stacking pillows from Flam's bed behind Mary until she was in a sitting position.

At the movement, and the strong fragrance emanating from her chest, the queen seemed to rouse slightly, and her eyelids fluttered.

Libby gasped. Could it be working already? With renewed energy, she held the drink to the queen's lips, and dribbled a tiny amount into her mouth. Little by little, drop by drop, somehow the queen swallowed about half a cup of the herbal tea, before growing heavy in Libby's arms again.

With the pot of tea set safely on the dresser, Libby re-arranged the pillows until the queen lay peacefully. But something had changed.

Instead of lying there immobile and senseless, the queen now seemed to be merely *asleep*. In a deep sleep, 'twas true, but there was somehow more *life* about her, if that was possible. *Mayhap 'tis just my imagination.* But Libby wanted it to be true, wanted Robert's potions to have helped the queen.

She chewed her lip, then ducked out of the room and hid the pot behind the drape again. *Time will tell.* And it would not be long till Ebba returned from dinner. But Libby was due to watch the queen again at dawn. She could hardly wait.

CHAPTER 12

SUNDAY 20TH OCTOBER 1566

MARY's STOMACH HURT, her head ached and her throat was as dry as a saut buckie. But more than anything, she needed to get away from that awful smell. "Open a window!" she croaked.

"Your Grace! You're awake!"

Forcing her gritty eyes open, Mary saw that Libby Logan sat beside her, and that she lay in the small bedchamber she used in the Kerr's tower house in Jedburgh. With a shaky arm, she pointed at the window. "The smell," she said, "open the window."

In a trice, Libby had done as she commanded, and blessedly fresh air flooded into the room.

Mary took a deep breath, filling her lungs. But still her eyes watered with the acrid aroma, and her nose wrinkled in disgust.

Libby dipped a linen cloth into a bowl on the oak dresser. "Let me sponge the salve off, ma'am. That will get rid of more of the smell."

While Libby ministered to her, Mary questioned the lady-in-waiting and discovered that she had lain unconscious for more than a day.

"How fare you now?" Libby asked, her brow crinkling.

"Everything 'urts," Mary answered succinctly. Then her insides cramped violently, and she waved a hand at Libby. "Quickly…

pass the bowl."

It took until she'd vomited several times before her stomach finally settled. And now she felt spent, and cold. She wriggled further under the bedcovers.

"Are you recovered, ma'am? Do you need the bowl any longer?"

Mary shook her head.

Libby smoothed the queen's hair away from her face, a look of concern on her face. Then she put the back of her hand against Mary's forehead. "You must be improved, for your fever appears to have broken." She stood up. "If you could wait a few minutes, I'll bring you a ginger and elderflower draught which should make you feel better."

A short time later, Mary frowned at Libby through the steam that rose from the soothing herbal tea. "Is this from Lusgerie?"

"'Tis from the doctor," Libby replied evasively.

"The doctor," Mary repeated slowly, and raised her eyebrows at the girl.

Libby's cheeks coloured, and she dropped her gaze. "From Monsieur Nau. My humble apologies, ma'am. You were so ill, and nothing Lusgerie prescribed was helping. So…" she swallowed. "So I went to see the French physician. He gave me some herbs, and that is what woke you," she finished in a rush.

"Some herbs?" Mary's eyebrows reached further towards her hairline.

"Aye, the salve on your chest to wake you, some cooling herbs for a compress, and the ginger and elderflower for your spleen."

"And what did Lusgerie prescribe?"

"He bled you, the first day. Then he had us sponge you with cold water against the fever."

There was a moment's silence. Mary frowned. "Nothing more?"

Libby shook her head.

"And he left *you* to look after me, rather than attending to me himself?"

"Not just me. The Maries too—we all take turns. 'Twas my turn this morning."

Mary scowled. Lusgerie was doubtless sitting, even now, at the Spread Eagle, with a goblet of brandy at his elbow. *What do I pay him for? I shall have to ask George Seton to find him a bed here, so he is readily on hand. But I will need to instruct cook to lock away the Armagnac. The man is a sot.*

~

Monday 21st October

Word quickly spread around town that the queen was improved, and Robert felt a swell of pride. *Mayhap 'twas the remedies I gave to Libby.* But he couldn't be sure if Libby had even been able to treat the queen. It niggled at him, even as he prepared a draught for McMann, who had contracted a dry cough since arriving in the Borders. *I may never know.*

But Robert found out the answer sooner than he expected.

Later that morning, a messenger arrived from Hartrigge House, requesting his presence 'at his earliest convenience'. Was the message from Libby or the queen? Or someone else—Lusgerie even?

Robert paced his room, wondering why he was being summoned, and debating whether he should change into the new outfit Claude had him buy. But his customary black fustian and dark leather was serviceable, and suitable for this time of day. *I should keep the brown for more formal occasions.*

With his mind made up, he grabbed his cloak and hat, strode off across the town, and was soon being ushered into the great hall of the tower house.

Arrayed around the wide stone fireplace

like a bouquet of flowers were the queen's ladies, needlework on their laps and small talk on their lips. Inevitably, his gaze was drawn to Libby, the most beautiful rose of all. Today she wore a russet red gown over a damask kirtle, and her hair glowed golden like barley under the summer sun. It took him a moment to recover himself and remember his manners. He swept off his hat and bowed low. "Good morrow, my ladies."

"Monsieur Nau!" Ebba Seton leapt up to greet him. "Most kind of you to join us. The queen wishes to see you." She beckoned to Libby. "Lady Preston will take you to her."

That will not help me get over my infatuation, thought Robert, even as his spirits soared at the thought of spending a few moments alone with her.

It took his men a day to make the litter, and two days to get him to Jedburgh, but finally Bothwell made it to Hartrigge House. Every hoof-beat of the journey had sent a jolt through his spine until the scar on his forehead throbbed, and the wound in his side ached so badly he had to clench his teeth not to cry out in pain. But, however bad it got, he would *not* show his weakness before his men.

And now, finally, they were here. He called his page over. "Paris, go get me an urgent audience with the queen." It irked him greatly to have to wait, but it would have annoyed him even more if the queen had been so poorly guarded that anyone—even one of her Privy Council—could just turn up at her house and gain access to her chamber.

While he waited for Paris to return, he gave orders to the captain of his guard. "Get a chair, and two men who can carry me in to see the queen. Then go and arrange lodgings for us. Try the Black Bull."

~

Robert followed Libby up the spiral staircase to the queen's room, admiring the grace of her posture and the elegant way her fingers trailed up the rope banister.

"I'm sorry you had to misdirect Master Somerville," whispered Libby, once they were out of earshot of the others.

Robert frowned. "Master Somerville?"

"Hugh. Outside. The other night."

"Ah!" *The pompous ass.* "I misdirected him?"

"About your position with the ambassador."

Robert waved a hand at her. "C'est rien." Then his jaw tightened at the memory and he locked eyes with her. "How was your walk?"

"Oh, I didn't go." She lifted a shoulder. "I told him I must sit with the queen."

Robert arched an eyebrow, even as relief washed away the envy he had felt moments before. "But he seemed such a pleasant man. And rich too."

Libby pressed her lips together. "Mayhap. But he was not first in line when they were handing out brains."

At this, Robert let out a peal of laughter. *I had not thought her to be amusing.* But they had reached the queen's bedchamber, and there was no further opportunity for chatter.

Knocking lightly on the timber door, Libby peeked inside. "Ma'am, 'tis Monsieur Nau, as you requested."

Mary waved them in. "Monsieur Nau, thank you for coming." She waved him up from his bow. "I 'ear I have you to thank for 'ealing me from my fever?"

Without all her finery, the Scots queen's sallow skin was more obvious, and the lines etched on her face by pain spoke more to Robert as a doctor than any words she could say. *She is not a well woman. Lusgerie could surely do more.* But he kept his expression neutral. "Oh, 'twas nothing, Your Grace. Merely a few herbs."

"A few 'erbs!" Mary gave a mirthless chuckle. "That smell was enough to waken the dead!"

"Ah! You refer to the salt of hartshorn? 'Tis… an acquired taste," he said, with a twitch of his cheek.

The queen pursed her lips, but she had a twinkle in her eye. "Mayhap. Now," she flicked a finger at Libby, "Lady Preston, fetch me the briarwood casket from the windowsill if you please."

A moment later, Mary had opened the brass lock on the polished casket and pulled out a small velvet pouch. "For you, monsieur, as a thank-you for your skills as a physician, and as recompense for your…" she made a face, "foul salts."

Robert's jaw dropped. From the weight of the purse she handed him, it contained more than a few gold coins. "Ma'am, you do not need to—"

"Nonsense!" The queen flicked a hand. "'Tis the least I could do. Were it not for you, Moray could even now be ordering my grave-cloth." Then she looked from Robert to Libby, a calculating look on her face. "Methinks young Lady Preston looks a trifle peaky. Some fresh air would do her good. Monsieur Nau," she gestured for Robert to leave the room, "pray take Lady Preston for a turn around the gardens. And send Lady Fleming to keep me company."

CHAPTER 13

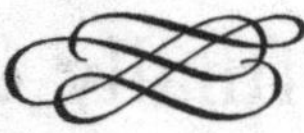

MONDAY 21ST OCTOBER

I AM *POPULAR* this *morning,* thought Mary, as there was another knock on the door of her bedchamber. "Enter!" she called, and was surprised to see Paris, the earl of Bothwell's manservant.

"Your Grace," Paris bowed low.

"Bonjour, Paris. Do you come from the earl?"

"Oui madame. 'E waits outside."

The earl must be recovered from his wounds. "Send 'im up."

In the intervening minutes before Bothwell

knocked at her door, there were some strange noises from the stairwell—scuffling and cursing and scraping. *What goes on?* It sounded like they were playing hand ba' out there.

When the earl finally entered, instead of the ostentatious bow she had come to expect from her trusted lieutenant, he merely bobbed his head and shoulders. "Your Grace."

"Lord Bothwell. Thank you for your visit. Are you fully healed?"

Bothwell grimaced. "Only a little better than when you visited last week, ma'am. The stab wound in my side burns like a hot poker and I can't walk more than a few steps. But when I heard you were ill, I had to come. My men took me in a horse litter." A look of disgust crossed his face. "A contraption of the devil, if ever there was one."

"How then did you manage the stairs?"

He set his jaw. "Carried in a chair."

Which explains the strange noises. "Per'aps you should sit." Mary motioned to the small chair beside her bed.

Once sat down, Bothwell looked less uncomfortable, although his complexion was still grey and there were new lines inscribed on his cheeks. He had lost weight, too, since last she saw him. "But, Your Grace, the object of my visit was to enquire after your health. I heard you were unconscious and had a fever."

"Had," Mary replied with emphasis. "The doctor cured me." She gave him a sideways look. "Mayhap you should have him look at your wound too."

"Lusgerie?"

"Non. Monsieur Robert Nau. The ambassador's physician. Perchance you passed him on the stair?"

"An olive-skinned man? All in black? With a young lady?"

"Oui." She tilted her head. "Paris could fetch him for you?"

Out in the quiet of the garden, with only the harsh craws of a couple of rooks to break the silence, Libby found that her shyness had returned, and she could think of nothing to say. Instead, she walked with her shoulders hunched and her eyes on the ground. *Why did the queen make us go for a walk? I should be avoiding the Frenchman, not seeking his company.*

But Robert had other ideas. With a touch to her elbow, he proffered his arm, then led her down the garden towards the river. "I run along here most mornings," he said, indicating the riverside path at the other side of the garden wall.

"Run?" Libby was so surprised by this

statement that it startled her out of her silence.

"Oui. 'Tis good for the body," he knocked a fist on the hard muscle of his thigh, then turned her to face him, his voice softer, "and for the mind." He gave her a searching look. "The queen was right. You appear tired."

'Tis no wonder. My dreams are filled with dark-haired Frenchmen, cut-throat reivers and dying queens. She lifted a shoulder. "I worry about Her Grace and don't sleep so well."

Robert's brows pinched together. "I can give you a draught of valerian. But my valise is at the inn. Will you walk with me?"

But before Robert could escort Libby from the garden, there was a shout, and a small, shrew-faced man ran up to them. Protectively, Robert stepped in front of Libby, his hand flying instinctively to the hilt of his sword.

"Monsieur Nau?" the man swept the cap from his head and bowed. "Forgive me for the intrusion. I am Nicholas Hubert. The earl of Bothwell sent me."

"Bonjour," Robert replied, his heart rate returning to normal. "How can I help you?"

"The queen suggested you might be able to help. The earl sustained an injury some two weeks past. His wound still bothers him."

Robert nodded slowly. If the queen recommended him, his reputation would grow. *Mayhap there will be more coin to earn, and my dream of a hospital in Paris will be a step closer.* "I will need to examine him. Where might I find him?"

"Right now, he is with the queen. We have not secured lodgings yet, but he hopes to room at The Black Bull."

Robert turned to Libby. "Might I be able

to examine him here, do you think? 'Twould be easier, since the earl is already at the tower house."

Libby looked from Robert to the tower house and back again, then seemed to come to a decision. "I will ask," she said, and hurried off across the garden.

Following more slowly, Robert fell into step beside Hubert. "And where are you from, monsieur?"

"France. Paris. Round here, they call me 'French Paris'. So original!" he said with a Gallic shrug.

"Moi aussi! I only recently arrived in Scotland. How long have you been here?"

"Too long," replied Hubert. "Years." He turned sharp eyes on Robert. "I miss Paris. 'ow was she when you left?"

"Noisy. Dirty. Overcrowded. But enchanting."

Hubert nodded sadly. "That is the Paris I

remember." He sighed. "I 'ope to get back one day."

"As do I," agreed Robert.

Back inside the tower house, they found Bothwell in the tiny guard room, across the stair from the queen's chamber. Robert eyed him cautiously. The man was notorious in these parts and had come up more than once in conversations with the ambassador. A good six inches shorter than Robert and perhaps ten years older, he was thickset and muscular, with short-cropped hair, a dark moustache, and a glower to match any he'd yet seen in Scotland.

"Doctor Nau," Hubert introduced him with a flourish.

Robert bowed low. "Lord Bothwell."

"I hear you healed the queen," Bothwell said without preamble.

"I gave some herbs, which seemed to help." Robert chose his words carefully.

"Herbs," Bothwell repeated, his mouth in a line. "Do you not favour bloodletting?"

"If warranted, yes. It can be a help if the humors are out of balance."

Bothwell narrowed his eyes. "My physician has bled me three times now. And still this wound will not heal."

"May I have a look?"

Jerking his chin at his manservant, Bothwell flicked a finger at his waist. "Help me with my doublet, Paris."

Hubert busied himself with the lacings that attached Bothwell's hose to his velvet outer garments, then lifted the earl's linen shirt to expose his belly.

Mon Dieu!

With the gash on his side revealed, Robert could understand why the earl seemed so ill-tempered, and he gained a new-found respect for the man's bravery. Red, angry skin surrounded the wound, and it was hot to the touch. *And painful*, judging from the way the earl winced when Robert probed the wound with his fingertips. "We need to reduce the heat and inflammation, my lord."

Bothwell merely grunted.

"Hubert," Robert addressed the earl's manservant, "can you send a man to the Carter's Rest and ask Monsieur McMann to send my valise? It has the herbs I need. And ask the kitchen to send up a bowl of boiling water, a jar of honey and some clean cloths."

While they waited, the earl seemed disinclined to talk, but the supplies from the kitchen arrived quickly, so Robert busied himself with cleaning Bothwell's wound and steeping some cloths in the hot water.

When his case arrived, he pulled out a small bowl, then mixed up a paste of honey, calendula and turmeric. When the poultice was ready, he spread it between two pieces of heated linen before applying it to the wound.

Bothwell flinched, but Robert ignored him and wound a bandage around the man's torso, tightly enough to keep the poultice in place.

"Now," Robert got the earl's attention. "You will need to keep this on overnight, my lord. I will visit on the morrow and apply a fresh compress." He glanced at Hubert. "The Black Bull?"

The manservant nodded.

Robert handed the earl some ground willow-bark. "It will take a few days for the wound to improve. But take a spoonful of this every four hours as an herbal tea, and you should receive some relief."

Bothwell gave a curt nod. "My thanks for your attentions."

Quickly, Robert tidied away his things— but not before looking out some valerian, and stowing it in a twist of paper.

Back at the fire once more with the other ladies, Libby kept her gaze averted and her hands busy with needlework. With Flam away keeping company with the queen, Libby might escape an interrogation—or teasing—but it was not unknown for Beth Beaton and the other ladies to indulge in gossip, so she tried to make herself as inconspicuous as possible.

Her plan worked for some length of time, until the door of the banqueting hall opened, and a dark-clad man was shown into the room. *Robert.*

He bowed. "Lady Preston, if it please you, could I speak with you for a moment?"

Libby froze in indecision. If she took him outside that would lead to speculation she could do without. But, depending on what he had to say, they might provoke just as much gossip if she spoke to him in here. *I will have to trust to his discretion.*

Setting down her sewing, Libby beckoned him over to the window where they might get at least a modicum of privacy. Aware that curious eyes were on her, she tried to keep her expression neutral.

With his back to the other ladies, Robert handed her a little package. "Valerian, as I promised. Take a pinch steeped in hot water half an hour before bed. And—" he held her eye as he handed her the powder, "I also recommend daily exercise to help you sleep. A walk, or a ride. 'Tis a good way to build an appetite, and you will rest better at night."

"I—I thank you, sire." Libby tucked the package into the pocket in her skirts. "But I cannot think when I might have time for a walk. We have to be ready to attend the queen at any moment."

Robert rubbed his chin. "'Tis similar with the ambassador." He gave her a significant look. "'Tis why I run at dawn."

CHAPTER 14

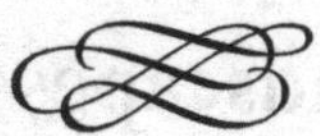

TUESDAY 22ND OCTOBER

THE REGULAR BEAT of his footsteps on the riverbank path had a calming effect, allowing Robert's mind to roam free. He loved that about running, just as he loved this time of day. With the dew rising from the water-meadows as morning mist, landmarks were reduced to indistinct brown shadows, and everything sparkled with the promise of a new day. It was almost magical.

Each day Robert went a slightly different route, exploring the hills and glens around

Jedburgh. And each day he found stunning scenery that made his heart beat faster and filled his eyes with delight.

Scotland is so different from France. The wild and open landscapes he'd seen here in the Borders contrasted markedly with the more pastoral countryside of France. And the people were different too—he'd seen little evidence of the showy excesses that were so prevalent at the French court, nor had he witnessed the deprivations and squalor of the capital city. Somehow, the people here seemed more *real*; like they were a part of the country—and each other—compared with the more insular focus of the French population.

Mayhap I am falling a little in love with Scotland, he thought as he rounded a corner and came within sight of the town once more. *Or a particular Scots lass.* His steps faltered.

As if the mere thought of her had conjured her presence, ahead of him on the bank of the river was the silhouette of the very woman who filled his thoughts. *Libby.*

"Good morrow." He drew to a stop beside her and swept into a low bow.

"Monsieur Nau. Hello." Libby's cheeks were flushed. Whether 'twas from the cold, the exertion, or from the sight of him, Robert could not be sure. She gestured at the path. "I took your advice."

"So I see." Robert fell into step beside her. "However, if you walk alone, you should probably not stray too far from the town." He caught her eye. "For safety."

"But the other ladies are still a-bed. And if I wish to exercise, this is my only real chance."

And I had vowed to try and avoid you.

Robert nodded. "'Tis worth trying for a few days. And if it helps you sleep, then we could look for a more permanent solution. But until then, I could accompany you if you wish? I can meet you from my morning run," he pointed at the track ahead, "like now."

~

And I had vowed to try and avoid you, thought Libby. But Robert was right; 'twas not safe for a lady to stray far on her own, and Libby had first-hand experience of how dangerous the Borders could be. However, when she'd awoken before dawn this morning, a walk had seemed like a good idea.

She pursed her lips. "For a few days," she agreed. "But if anyone sees us, we will need to cease meeting like this, for there will be gossip."

He sucked in a breath. "Oui. And did you try a valerian draught last night?"

"Aye. It tastes like… mud." She made a face. "I am sorry to say."

Robert laughed. "Make sure not to steep

it too long in the hot water before you drink. But did it help you to sleep?"

She raised a shoulder. "Mayhap."

He nodded slowly. "Try it for a few more days." With a sideways look, he added, "Doctor's orders."

~

Bothwell hated to admit it, but the treatment given the previous day by the French doctor had reduced his pain, and let him sleep better. He grimaced. *What sleep I managed.*

The Black Bull might be one of the better-appointed inns in the town, but it was a popular drinking-place, and there were many lords, gentlemen and soldiers attending the queen who found distraction in its barrels of ale and casks of whisky. Until all hours of the night…

But now it was morning, and Nau attended him, peeling off the poultice he'd applied yesterday.

The physician nodded with satisfaction. "Bon. The inflammation has reduced, I think." He looked at the earl. "Do you have less pain?"

"Yes." Bothwell admitted, though it galled him to do so. For if the man healed him, he would need paying—and Bothwell had already paid the physician he'd left behind at Hermitage Castle. *The one who left me writhing in agony.* He ground his teeth.

With a warm cloth, Nau wiped the wound site clean, then motioned to Paris to hand him the new compress he had prepared.

Monsieur Nau had almost finished securing the bandage when there was a frantic banging at the door. "Doctor, doctor!"

Paris looked to the earl for guidance.

But Bothwell already had his dagger in his hand and had shooed the doctor out of the way. He jerked his chin at the door. "Open it."

His hand on his sword hilt, Paris admitted the messenger. "What is the meaning of this interruption?"

"My lords, forgive me." The page bowed low. "But 'tis the queen. She has fallen ill again, and they sent me to fetch the French doctor."

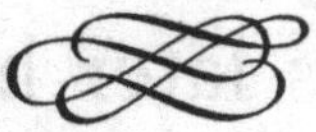

CHAPTER 15

BY THE TIME Robert left Bothwell and arrived at Hartrigge House, he found Lusgerie in the process of bleeding the queen, who lay motionless on her small bed.

"Monsieur Nau." Lusgerie gave him no greeting, merely a hard stare. "What brings you here?"

"Doctor Lusgerie." Robert dipped his head. "The ladies sent for me. I am sorry to hear the queen is unwell again. Can I do anything to help?"

Scratching his red-veined nose, Lusgerie grunted, "Go to the kitchen and get me some hot water."

Robert clenched his teeth, but said nothing. Some minutes later he returned with a pottery jug.

"And now I need some bandages," was Lusgerie's next demand.

He treats me like a servant, thought Robert as he hurried down the stair again.

But on the way back up he was intercepted by Mary Seton. "Doctor Nau! I hadn't heard that you'd arrived. How is Her Grace?"

Robert blew out an exasperated sigh. "I wish I knew. Lusgerie is bleeding her, and he sends me on errands like a pageboy."

Ebba put her hands on her hips. "That will not do." She held out a hand for the bandages. "Go sit with the ladies," she inclined her head towards the banqueting hall behind them, "and I will take these to Lusgerie and get rid of him as soon as he is done."

Robert bowed when he entered the great hall. As usual, the ladies were grouped around the fire, which burned brightly against the autumn chill. Heavy tapestries lined the walls and thick drapes were tied back from the windows. "Good morrow, gentle ladies. My lady Seton said for me to join you while she…" he searched for the right word, "deals with Monsieur Lusgerie."

At the far side of the hearthside Libby had her head down, concentrating on her sewing. *Or mayhap she avoids looking at me to avert any gossip.*

"Come, sit." Flam motioned him over to a chair. "How is the queen?"

Truth or tact? Robert didn't like to speak ill of a fellow physician, but Lusgerie didn't make that easy. "Lusgerie is with her right now, so I have not examined her. Lady Seton will let me know when he is finished." He removed his jerkin and sat in the proffered seat by the fire. "The message I got said that Her Grace had fallen ill again?"

This time Beth Beaton answered. "Yes, she complained of her spleen again this morning, and then she swooned. That's when we sent for you."

"I thank you for the compliment, but 'tis difficult when she already has a physician. I do not wish to offend him."

Beth's mouth twisted. "We heard that your treatment had improved Lord Bothwell. And Lusgerie seems to do little for the queen. We hoped that another approach..." she tailed off with a shrug.

"You said she swooned." Robert leaned forward. "Was there anything obvious that would cause her to lose consciousness? An upset? A fright?"

The ladies glanced at each other, and then Flam answered for them. "She had a letter from the French King, with news from his spies about Lord Darnley, and how he plots to raise a Catholic army from Spain and take the Scottish throne. 'Twas after she read his missive that she fell ill."

"'Tis Lord Darnley's fault, to be sure," declared Mary Livingston.

"She worries about Lord Darnley constantly," added Beth. "And about her half-brother Moray, who wishes to be regent. And about her cousin Queen Elizabeth, who supports the Protestant lords." She gave an elegant shrug. "There is much to worry about when you are a queen, and all around you are conniving men who grasp for power."

And all that anxiety will affect her health. "It seems that she has much cause for melancholy. And that can cause issue with the spleen."

After about twenty minutes, Mary Seton reappeared in the banqueting room. "Lusgerie is gone," she said, with a roll of her eyes. "Monsieur Nau, would you like to examine the queen now?"

"Of course." Robert stood up and collected his valise from where he'd left it by the door. "Would one of you ladies be able to assist?"

He held his breath, hoping that Libby would volunteer. For if he was to see her in the mornings by the riverside, there was no point in trying to avoid her now. He knew he had no fortune, and could not compete with a noble like Hugh Somerville for her heart. But perhaps if she spent enough time with him, she would come to admire him, to have feelings for him. For he assuredly had feelings for her, which only grew stronger each time he saw her.

But Libby didn't volunteer. She was nominated.

"My Lady Preston," Flam arched an eyebrow. "You were so useful to the doctor last time. I'm sure he would appreciate your help again this time."

~

Libby looked up from her sewing and caught the speculative look on Flam's face. *What is she up to?* "Would nobody else like to help? I'm not the only one who can help the doctor."

"'Twill let us catch up on our sewing," Flam said with a wave of her hand. "You're so quick and so neat, you put us to shame. Now, go sit with the queen. I'll relieve you after lunch."

Robert was strangely silent as they ascended the stairs to the queen's room, but when they got there, he had her open the drapes and then the window. "To stop our eyes from watering so much at the smell," he said as he pulled a pot of the pungent salve from his valise.

With the potion held under the queen's nose, this time it took just minutes for her to awaken.

"How do you feel, ma'am?" Robert asked.

"My stomach 'urts," Mary replied with a groan. "It feels like someone wears 'eavy boots and spins round and around in my insides."

Robert frowned. "May I?" he held his hands over the queen's abdomen.

Mary nodded.

Pulling down the bedcovers so the queen was covered only by her chemise, Robert used the flats of his fingers to palpate her belly.

"Is it my spleen?" the queen asked, her green eyes filled with concern.

His mouth in a line, Robert straightened.

"I think we need to make you vomit. Libby," he gave her a look that made her heart flutter, "could you please fetch a bowl, a jug of wine and a cup?"

Libby hurried downstairs to the kitchen and soon returned with the items he'd requested.

Into a cup of wine, Robert mixed a teaspoon of strong-smelling powder and proffered it to the queen. "Drink it please, ma'am. Hold your nose if the odour is too much for you."

It took two cups before the emetic had the desired effect and the queen lay back on her pillows, the lines of worry on her face smoothed.

Robert took the bowl away from her, then blanched when he glanced at the contents. Motioning Libby over, he turned his back so the queen couldn't see what he was doing. Then he pointed into the bowl, at a strange green substance amongst the other contents of the queen's stomach.

Libby's hand flew to her mouth, stifling a gasp.

With the tiniest of nods, Robert swivelled his eyes at the door, then stood. "Ma'am, Libby will show me where to dispose of this. We shall return momentarily."

Out in the stairwell, Libby touched Robert's arm. "What *is* that?" she whispered.

Robert grimaced. "Not here. Come." He set off down the stairs and led Libby into the garden. "We should dispose of this on the midden," he said when they were out in the open air.

"The stables are down here," Libby pointed to her left.

Before he emptied the bowl, Robert produced a small dagger, and retrieved a sample of the abnormal emissions, which he placed in a small container. "I shall test this later," he said, with a grim expression.

"But what do you think it is?" Libby asked. "Is it the queen's spleen?"

He looked deep into her eyes, which caused her pulse to quicken once more. "No," he said, his voice grave. "I think it is poison."

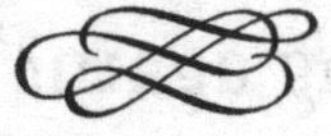

CHAPTER 16

AT ROBERT's WORDS, Libby gasped, and her eyes widened. "But—who would do such a thing? Everyone loves the queen, do they not?"

Robert hated to alarm Libby, but it was important that she realised the danger the queen was in—the danger they were *all* in. "From what the Maries were saying earlier, she has enemies from amongst her lords—and even her husband the king plots against her. So any one of them could be the culprit."

His shoulders tensed as if a great weight descended on them. "We may never know."

"But if we don't know who did it, how can we protect the queen? How can we prevent this happening again?"

A very good question. Robert wiped his dagger clean on a handful of straw, giving himself a moment to think. "The poison must have been hidden in something she ate." He frowned. "Who would have access to the queen's food?"

Libby pursed her lips. "Cook and the kitchen staff. And the serving staff."

"Any one of whom could be bribed to turn their back, or to add something to the queen's dishes."

"True. But I think cook can be trusted. She's worked for the queen for years—she'd have no reason to change her loyalties now."

For enough money, most people can be bought. The tavern gossip in Paris had been full of scandals in the French court which would attest to that. *But there might be a way to solve this.* "We shall speak to this cook then. If she knows that we suspect poisoning, she will know that she will be chief suspect, should the queen sicken again. For we shall tell her that from now on no servants are to serve the queen or touch her food, and that you will deliver all the queen's meals personally."

~

Wednesday 23rd October
After a third treatment by the ambassador's physician, Bothwell's wound was so much improved that he was able to walk, unaided, into the room at the Spread Eagle where the privy council was to meet.

On the first floor of the inn, the banqueting room was spacious and warm, with its roaring fire, thick tapestry hangings and oak-panelled floor. It was also convenient for the earl of Moray and many of Mary's senior lords, who resided at the inn. The queen would also have stayed there, but a fire on her first night in Jedburgh had driven her away and into the Kerr's tower house.

Lord Moray was to preside over the meeting, much to Bothwell's disgust, since the queen was still recovering from the illness she'd contracted on her return from Hermitage.

And Moray revelled in the chance to step into Mary's shoes, even if just for a day. "Maitland," he ordered, "write a missive to His Majesty the king of France saying that his sister-in-law the queen of Scots has been ill these six days with fits of vomiting and dwams of swooning which put some men in fear of her life. But say that she is now much improved, sleeps well and soundly, and we see no tokens of death."

Maitland smoothed a large piece of paper on the table before him and pulled out his quill. "We see no tokens of death," he repeated slowly, and fixed Moray with a baleful gaze.

Moray's eyes narrowed slightly, but he made no other reaction. "Exactly," he said. "We would not wish to give their majesties any cause for concern."

Something goes on between those two, thought Bothwell. *I will need to get Paris to go a-spying, to see if he can find out what it is.*

CHAPTER 17

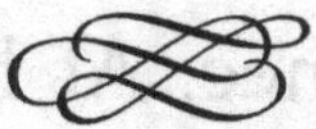

FRIDAY 25TH OCTOBER

MARY PICKED AT a loose thread on her bedspread. "And the crown must pass to my son James, not to his father the king. To my 'alf-brother James Stewart, Earl of Moray, I entrust the principal part of the government and give him charge of the prince."

Dictating her final wishes like this made Mary's heart feel hollow, and a well of sadness lay close to the surface. But her illness of the last few days, when she had lain unconscious for much of the time, had made her realise that she should make provision for the young prince, and for her country.

At her bedside, her secretary Maitland sat on a small chair with a portable writing desk propped on his knee. At her last statement, his quill stopped scratching and he turned beady eyes on her. "You are sure, ma'am?"

Mary sighed. "Who else can I trust? Darnley is… not the man I thought 'e was. Per'aps Elizabeth's favourite, Lord Dudley, would 'ave made me a better marriage. For Darnley—" and then she stopped herself. *My illness makes me speak rashly. I should be more circumspect around Maitland, for he may yet be in league with the Protestant lords.*

"Your marriage to Lord Darnley…" Maitland spoke even more carefully than usual, "is not what you would wish?"

Mary's shoulders tensed. "I… No. He is not the husband I would wish. But, unlike my grandfather, Henry, I believe in the sanctity of marriage. So I must remain attached to Lord Darnley, even if he *is* most unsuitable as a king."

Maitland touched his bottom lip with the end of his quill. "If you wish, ma'am, we could seek annulment of the marriage on account that your dispensation from the Pope for consanguinity arrived *after* your wedding ceremony. Lord Darnley *is* your cousin after all."

Decisively, Mary shook her head. "I cannot petition for an annulment, for that would leave Prince James illegitimate."

"Hmmm." While he deliberated, the fingers of Maitland's left hand tapped rhythmically against his thumb, as if he heard a melody that was inaudible to anyone else, or played an invisible musical instrument. After a full minute, he seemed to reach a decision. "Ma'am, I will speak with your council and we will find the means that you shall be quit of him without prejudice to your son. Leave the matter with me and worry you not."

Mary's heart leapt. "You will speak to the Pope?"

Her secretary held up a finger. "Leave it with me."

~

Even though his progress up the turnpike stair in Hartrigge House was laborious, Bothwell marvelled at the change in his condition after just a few days under the care of the ambassador's physician. 'Twas only on Monday that he had to be carried up these same stairs.

Now he managed on his own, albeit on the arm of his servant Paris. Perhaps Nau would take employment in his household. Bothwell frowned. *But could I afford him?* His modern ideas might not come cheaply.

On the first-floor landing, Bothwell paused for a minute to catch his breath. While he stood there, the earl of Moray passed on his way to the ground floor, at a pace which brought home to Bothwell just how much healing he still had to do.

He glared at the empty stairwell, angry at the earl for making him feel like an old man. His fists clenched. 'Twill *be some time before I am well enough to run like that, or to ride.* But ride he must, as soon as the queen was ready to resume her progress through the Borders. For schemers like Moray could easily usurp Bothwell's position as the queen's most trusted minister, and that would disrupt his plans to get closer to the throne. *I cannot allow that.*

"Wait outside," he instructed Paris when they finally reached the queen's room. "Stay alert."

"Ah!" Mary greeted him when he entered. "First my lord Moray, and now my lord Bothwell. I am blessed with the most auspicious company tonight!" She sat in her bed wearing a blue brocade partlet over her white chemise and supping on a bowl of broth.

Bothwell bowed stiffly. "Your Grace."

Mary motioned him to the chair beside her bed, and he sat down gladly.

"Forgive me if I carry on eating my potage. I 'ave been so busy today there 'as been little time to eat."

"Of course, ma'am." Bothwell cleared his throat. "I shall not keep you long."

Taking another spoonful of the soup, Mary motioned for him to keep talking.

"Ma'am, with your interests at heart, I have had my man Paris listen to the gossip around the town. He has come across some information of grave import that I wanted to make you aware of."

Mary's eyes grew rounder. "Carry on."

Bothwell dropped his voice. "There is talk that the king is in Glasgow, and that he plots with the king of Spain to take your throne."

"I 'ad also 'eard that," Mary said, putting

the bowl aside. She looked him in the eye. "Now, more than ever, I 'ave need of my loyal lords such as you. Tell me you will support and defend me against the king, should it become necessary?"

"You have my word of honour, Your Grace. I will defend you to my last breath." He held up a hand. "But the other matter that I wanted to speak about is also related to your safety. There are reports that Moray and Maitland are scheming although I know not the subject of their plans. But I have seen evidence of their collusion with my own eyes, at our last privy council meeting."

Mary's face fell, and she pressed a palm into her chest. "Is there no-one I can trust?" she moaned. "Not even my own brother?"

"Half-brother," Bothwell corrected. *Time to put a nail in the bastard's coffin.* "One who has known what it is like to reign as regent, and may have designs on the throne once more."

The queen's skin, usually pale, turned white, and her breath quickened. "I… I cannot…" but she didn't finish the sentence. Instead she lay back on her pillows and closed her eyes.

Bothwell waited for a minute, thinking that Mary was just overcome with sorrow at his news. But when she made no movement, he put a hand on her arm.

"Your Grace." He gave her a little shake. "Are you awake?"

There was no response.

Panic rising in his chest, Bothwell staggered to the door and shouted on Paris. "Go fetch the French doctor! As fast as you can!"

CHAPTER 18

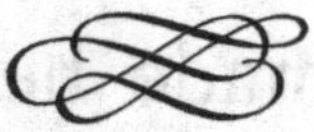

IT WAS UNUSUAL for Libby to have the banqueting room to herself, but she rather liked the peace and quiet, and not having to guard herself constantly against gossip.

Now that the queen was feeling better, even though still confined to her sick-bed, she held meetings with her lords which kept her busy for most of the afternoon, and left the ladies-in-waiting at a loose end. Beth and Livvy decided to visit with their husbands, and Ebba went to the church to give thanks. So, when Maitland suggested a visit to the town, Flam jumped at the opportunity to stretch her legs. But Libby, not wishing to play gooseberry, made her excuses and remained at the tower house.

And now she sat on her own, hairs prickling at the back of her neck and a chill running down her spine. For clattering footsteps echoed in the stairwell and panicked shouts came from the floor above. *Something is wrong.*

Could it be reivers? Her heart beat so loudly she was sure it could be heard outside in the street. But was that not Bothwell's voice? And there was only one set of footsteps on the stairs. *Mayhap the queen is in danger.*

Might the poisoner have found a way to circumvent the safeguards that she and Robert had put in place? Should they have told someone else, rather than trying not to worry the queen and cause gossip at court?

Heart in her mouth, Libby picked up a pair of scissors from the table—*just in case*—and hurried up the stairs to the queen's room, dreading what she might find there.

And what she found in the queen's bedchamber proved that her instincts were right. For Mary lay unconscious once more, with the earl of Bothwell by her side, holding her hand in both of his.

The earl's face—usually so proud and arrogant—was distraught. "Is the doctor here yet?"

Libby rushed to the end of the bed. "No. Have you sent for him?"

"Paris is away to fetch him."

"What happened? Her Grace had been feeling so much better."

"One minute we were talking, and then she swooned. I've been unable to waken her since."

"Wait here!" With a swirl of her skirts, Libby raced up the stairs to her room in the garret where she'd stowed the left-over salve.

A moment later, she arrived back in the queen's chamber and sat on Flam's bed, holding the container of pungent paste under Mary's nose, and fervently praying that Robert's salt of hartshorn would work once more.

But it had no effect this time. The queen lay senseless, even as the rank odour filled the room and made Libby's eyes water.

"Where is that cursed doctor?" the earl asked gruffly and hobbled across the timber floor to open a window.

He got his answer seconds later when the stairwell was filled with the sound of hurrying footsteps, and then Robert burst into the room, closely followed by Paris.

"At last!" cried the earl.

Libby was unable to stop the colour

rising in her cheeks at the sight of the Frenchman, for she had walked with him these last three mornings, and each day she had enjoyed his company more.

Robert had entertained her with stories from the ambassador's household, and anecdotes from his work at the hospital in Paris. But more than that, he had drawn her out about what it was like to live as part of the queen's court, and quizzed her about her childhood at Preston. Perhaps it was because he was French, but he was the first man she'd ever met who seemed more interested in what *she* had to say than in talking about himself or his business.

He makes me feel like I am important to him. And because he was someone her step-father would never consider as suitable, the time she spent with him was easy and uncompli-cated. So when she was with Robert she didn't have to worry about impressing a potential suitor or charming a high-born lord who might have younger, marriageable, sons. She could just be herself.

Why can Hugh Somerville not be interesting like Robert? It would make life so much easier if Master Somerville was even half as entertaining as the Frenchman. She might consider him then.

Oh! Libby's fingertips fluttered to her lips and her chest tightened. What was it she had decided when she arrived in Jedburgh? That she could learn to suffer the company of *any* man as long as he wasn't an ogre? And now she was comparing potential suitors to the doctor and finding them wanting. *That is not the way to go.* She must stop these foolish thoughts—and stop meeting Robert in the mornings. For she needed to focus on her purpose here.

But focus was difficult, when Robert turned his handsome brown eyes on her, making her insides melt, and asked in his bewitching French accent, "What happened here?"

After getting details of how the queen had fallen ill again, Robert thanked the earl for calling him so promptly. "Early medical attention might make all the difference," he said, his face grim. "Now, I must examine Her Grace."

Taking the earl's place on the chair by her bedside, he felt the queen's forehead —*clammy*; palpated her stomach—*too firm*; and then took hold of her wrist to check her pulse—*thready and slow*. Robert clenched his teeth. *This is not good.*

"The hartshorn has not worked this time," Libby said in a small voice, worry-lines creasing her forehead.

"Not yet." Robert gave what he hoped was a reassuring smile. "It can take some time. Perhaps you could rub it on her chest while I prepare some medicine?" Then he turned to the earl and his manservant, who hovered in the doorway.

"Monsieur Hubert, could you please bring us some candles? I fear 'twill be a long night."

"Of course!" Hubert hurried away.

"My lord, would you be able to find out for me what the queen has eaten today?"

Bothwell pointed at the bowl on the little table between the beds. "She was eating that soup just before she fell ill."

"Thank you." Picking up the bowl, Robert sniffed the remnants of broth. It gave off the tang of pepper and spices, but that was unsurprising. He then examined the soup, stirring it around with the spoon, and his eye was caught by a tiny piece of a waxy dark green substance. *A piece of leaf, maybe?* Not wishing to alarm—or alert—the earl, he set the bowl aside. *I shall take a sample later.*

Robert ducked his head to hide his face, and fiddled with his valise. But his mind was racing. If the queen had been poisoned again, could the earl be to blame? *But why would he send for me when Lusgerie is her physician?*

And if the earl was not to blame, then who was? Could the cook have gone against their instructions? He looked up again. "Lord Bothwell, do you know who delivered the queen's soup? Was it one of the servants?"

"She was already eating when I joined her. Lord Moray was with her before that. He might know the answer."

Robert nodded. "Could you please ask him? Once Hubert comes back."

Bothwell frowned. "Do you suspect the food is the cause?" His face blanched. "Or poison?"

"'Tis too early to say, sire. I am suspicious. But the more I know, the more helpful it will be when trying to cure Her Grace."

At that moment, Hubert arrived and handed the candles to Robert.

The earl motioned for his manservant to give him his arm. "Come, Paris. We need to go find the bastard, and give him a grilling."

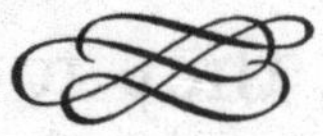

CHAPTER 19

THEY HAD ALMOST finished their slow descent of the stairs when Bothwell stopped. "Wait!" Paris looked at him questioningly.

"Before we look for Moray, we should question the kitchen staff. See who took the soup to the queen. Then we can see if the earl has the same story."

"Oui," Paris agreed. "Good idea."

And those ideas are why I am Lieutenant of the Borders, and you are merely my servant. But Bothwell kept his thoughts to himself. *For I still need the man to help me walk. No sense in antagonising him.*

In the ground-floor kitchen with its impressive vaulted ceiling and large ovens belching out heat, they found the red-faced cook.

"Soup?" she said, when they questioned her. "Aye. 'Twas Davie over there—" she pointed at a ginger-haired kitchen hand, "he took the soup to the queen. Davie!" she shouted him over. "'Twas you took the queen her broth earlier, was it not?"

"Aye. But no," Davie's cheeks reddened under the gaze of the two men. He took off his cap and scrunched it nervously in his hands. "I mean, I took the bowl. But the earl took it off me. The one with the dark hair," he said, holding a hand above his head to indicate a tall man. "Said he was going to visit the queen and would take it to her."

Bothwell pinned Davie with his steely gaze. "The earl of Moray?"

Visibly wilting under Bothwell's glare, the servant swallowed. "Aye. Moray."

Bothwell caught Paris' eye. *Interesting.* He nodded at the cook. "We shan't take up any more of your time. Good day."

~

Once the earl and Hubert had left, Libby put down the pot of salve, and voiced the question she had not been able to ask with the others present. "Is it poison again?"

Robert opened his hands. "I cannot say for sure. But she is gravely ill, and I fear the poisoner has tried again, since his—or her—last attempt failed." He reached down and pulled a small container from his valise. "And many poisons have a cumulative effect, so our job this time will be harder."

Time passed in a blur as Libby and Robert fought to save the queen's life. Her temperature had dropped alarmingly; her hands freezing and her feet and legs cold to the knees. Robert set Libby to rubbing the queen's hands, using a stimulant cream to lubricate and warm her skin. At the same time, he massaged her feet and legs, manipulating her limbs to encourage the blood flow.

After they had worked on the queen for nearly twenty minutes, Mary Seton tapped on the door and her eyes widened at the treatment they had resorted to. "Is this truly necessary?" she asked, her mouth down-turned and her long face serious. "'Tis very undignified for Her Grace."

Robert motioned her over. "Feel her feet."

Ebba touched the queen's toes, then recoiled with a gasp. "She's ice-cold!"

"Oui. And we need to restore heat or she will die."

"I'll send a servant to bank the fire. And..." Ebba looked from Libby to Robert, "have you eaten?"

"I'm not hungry," Libby replied. Her stomach churned with worry, and she couldn't imagine managing even a morsel of food. "But Robert might be?"

He shook his head.

"Is there anything else I can do?" Ebba asked, twisting a gold-enamelled ring on her right hand.

Robert paused in his ministrations. "Pray," he said. "And ask all the lords and ladies to pray also."

CHAPTER 20

BOTHWELL AND PARIS eventually found Moray in the salon of the Spread Eagle. "Let me do the questioning," Bothwell instructed, "but you keep your eyes and ears open, and see what you observe."

"I have grave news," Bothwell announced when they arrived at Moray's table.

Moray looked up from his quail eggs. "Yes?"

Was that a gleam in his eye? Bothwell dropped into a chair next to the earl. "The queen is ill again, and the doctor wonders if 'tis a bad reaction to her food. You were with her earlier this evening. How did she seem?"

"Well," Moray said, with a jut of his chin.

He is talkative this evening, Bothwell thought sourly. *Perhaps this will elicit more than a one-word answer.* "Do you remember, then, how she came by the broth she was eating?"

Moray's eyelids dropped, hooding his eyes. "Some servant perhaps—" he waved a hand dismissively. "Such matters are of little import to me. I cannot say."

Bothwell pushed him. "So, you don't remember who served her with the soup?"

A muscle twitched in Moray's jaw, but his face remained impassive. "No."

And some call me heartless. At least I am not also a liar. "You will be glad to hear that the doctor is with Her Grace even now." Bothwell stood to go, but couldn't resist a last dig at the earl. "Pray to our Lord for her healing.

For pity help us if Darnley was to take the throne."

~

After about an hour, darkness had descended, leaving Libby and Robert working by candlelight.

Mary's face gleamed palely in the flickering light, and Libby stopped her ministrations to place the back of a hand on the queen's forehead. "I think she is a little less cold," she said, and walked behind Robert to the dresser where, despite their protestations, Ebba had placed some nuts, sweetmeats, and a carafe of wine. Pouring two goblets of Bordeaux, Libby handed one to Robert.

"Merci."

"While we've been working," she said, "I've been thinking." Sat back on Flam's cot, Libby placed her wine beside Mary's prayer book on the tiny bedside table. "About the poisoner."

With a lift of his eyebrows, Robert encouraged her to continue.

"The other morning, when the queen first took sick, I was in the kitchen eating breakfast, and the earl of Moray came and took away porridge for the queen."

Robert's nostrils flared. "And tonight, Lord Bothwell visited with the queen immediately after Moray, and the queen was eating soup."

"Yes. And then she fell ill again."

"So, the earl of Moray was present both times."

"Exactly."

Robert narrowed his eyes. "Bothwell was also present tonight, so we cannot rule him out."

"But Bothwell didn't arrive in Jedburgh until two days after she first fell ill."

"Ah." A nerve twitched in Robert's jaw. "Then Moray is our main suspect."

"But he is the queen's brother. Half-brother," Libby corrected herself.

"And from what the ladies were saying, a half-brother who has designs on the throne."

Libby's skin chilled, as she tried to imagine her own brother doing this, and how someone could feel such rivalry or jealousy that they would resort to murder. "Surely he would not stoop to poisoning his sister?"

"Men have killed for far less. And from what the ambassador tells me, the queen was convinced she was also a target when her secretary Riccio got killed. Moray was never officially implicated in that murder, but du Croc is sure he was an instigator of the plot. For Riccio had too much influence with the queen and had usurped Moray's place as her advisor."

Libby nodded slowly. "We shall have to warn her."

"But first," Robert put down his wine and uncovered the queen's feet again, "we need to save her life. Or the poisoner will have won."

CHAPTER 21

IT WAS AFTER midnight before the queen had warmed enough for them to stop working on her hands and feet. Rather than seeming lifeless, Mary now appeared to sleep quietly, her breathing steadier and her heartbeat more regular.

Robert reached across and stilled Libby's hands. "I think we can stop now." He pointed a finger at the queen's face. "She is past the worst."

Rising from his seat at the end of Mary's

235

bed, Robert stretched his back for a moment, then went to the dresser and poured two cups of wine. He handed one to Libby, then sat beside her on Flam's narrow bed.

Libby sipped the wine gratefully. "Do you think she's recovered?" The end of her question was lost in a huge yawn. "I'm so sorry," she said when she finally recovered. "I'm just…"

But of course, by then, Robert had succumbed to the infectiousness of her yawn, and they both dissolved with mirth.

"We shouldn't laugh," Libby spluttered, recovering herself a little. "The queen is sick."

Robert lifted a shoulder. "We have worked hard for hours to restore her health. I think we deserve a moment of levity." His eyes twinkled. "Doctor's orders."

Her blue eyes were lustrous in the candlelight as she looked up at him, her lips slightly parted. "Thank you," she whispered.

Robert quirked his brow. "What for?"

"For helping my mistress. And for letting me help too. You..." she faltered, and dropped her gaze, a blush rising on her cheeks.

His breath held, Robert gently lifted her chin with his forefinger. "I...?" he prompted, with an encouraging tilt of his head.

"You are the first man to treat me," she lifted a shoulder, "more like an equal." She searched his eyes. "Like what I say is important to you. 'Tis unusual."

"But you *are* important to me." Robert's heart swelled. "More than you know." He locked his eyes on hers, then slowly lowered his head and brushed her lips, with a touch that was butterfly-light. "More than I could ever say."

Libby's breath caught, and her eyes darkened, but she didn't pull away. Instead, it was as if a magnetic attraction pulled her closer, surrounding him with the intoxicating vanilla scent of her skin.

Robert moved his hand to the angle of her jaw, then tilted her face towards him. When she didn't protest, he kissed her again, dropping the softest, sweetest caresses onto the bow of her lips, the tip of her nose, the angle of her chin. "You are so beautiful," he breathed.

She touched his hand, then looked deep into his eyes. "'Tis you who are beautiful."

He chuckled. "Handsome, surely?"

"Beautiful as a person. But, aye," her lips twitched, "handsome too."

Could she care for me? Running an arm around her slim waist, he pulled her closer, and this time he kissed her properly, crushing her to his chest and letting his lips tell of his feelings, of how she filled his dreams, captured his heart, and made him fall in love with her…

For the first time in her life, Libby felt what it was like to be kissed properly by a man. Not by one who only had his own pleasure in mind, but by a man who seemed intent solely on giving *her* pleasure.

His lips were so soft, so tender, and he seemed to know exactly how to use them to elicit the most enticing sensations. *And his tongue!* Very quickly, she discovered the delight that was to be found in allowing his tongue to tangle with hers, to tickle and tease the insides of her mouth, teeth and lips. It sent the most delightful tingle burning through her core and down to the very deepest part of her.

And then when his lips moved to the line of her jaw and rained the daintiest of kisses down the most sensitive parts of her neck, she thought she would melt with the exquisiteness of it.

Unable to resist, and intoxicated by the sandalwood scent of him, she put her arms around his strong back and tangled a hand in his hair.

With a groan, Robert moved his mouth back to cover hers, and deepened their kiss, so that Libby could think of nothing else save the feeling of his lips on hers, and the little rivulets of bliss that made her breath come faster, made her toes curl—and made her back spasm. With a wince, she pulled away from him.

"Is something amiss?" His face clouded with concern.

Libby rubbed the small of her back. "'Tis just… not the most comfortable position."

Robert eyed Flam's pillow. "We could lie down?"

Libby tensed, and all her old worries and fears came flooding back. "No!" She sprang to her feet, searching for a way to escape. But

Robert was between her and the door. "Let me—"

"What's wrong?" Robert looked distraught. "Libby, I…" He opened his hands. "I am so sorry if I upset you. But I could not bear to think that I might hurt you."

At his genuine contrition, Libby's panic subsided somewhat. She shook her head. "'Tis me, 'tis… memories. Bad memories. I—"

"Did someone hurt you?" Robert's hands were on her arms now, and he pulled her to him, enfolding her in his embrace and comforting her like a frightened horse. "Tell me who, and I shall challenge them to a duel."

Libby gave a sad smile. "There's no need. The perpetrator was hanged."

Robert pushed her to arm's length and searched her face. "Hanged?" A thousand thoughts seemed to flicker across his dark eyes, and his expression turned sombre. "Tell me—"

Libby shook her head. "I cannot tell you more."

Pulling her closer again, Robert smoothed a wisp of hair off her forehead, then tilted her chin with a finger and looked into her eyes. "Even after all we have shared?" His mouth pressed into a line. "Do you not trust me?"

She averted her gaze. "I…"

"Libby, look at me."

Reluctantly, she met his eyes.

He spoke solemnly, sincerity shining from his brown eyes. "Mon amour, there is nothing you could say or do that would change the way I feel about you. Nothing." Taking a deep breath, he continued, "I love you. I want nothing more than to spend every day of the rest of my life with you, showing you what it is to be loved and cherished and adored. For you deserve that. You are the most wonderful woman I have ever met, and you deserve a man who will love you. Properly."

Dropping to his knees, he took her hand. "I have no ring, for I did not plan this. But I will get one if only you will say yes. Libby Logan, will you marry me?"

Libby's free hand flew to her mouth, and tears welled in her eyes. "I… I cannot, Robert, I'm so sorry."

"But you care about me, do you not? Surely you would not have kissed me that way if you had no feelings for me?" As if to demonstrate the truth of his words, Robert got to his feet and dropped his mouth to hers, crushing her to him so that every inch of her pressed against his lean, muscular body.

The feel of him, so close, so solid, so *real*, kindled a desire that she had never known before, a fire that burned in the pit of her belly, sending heat coursing through every part of her body and sending her hands snaking around his neck to pull him closer, closer…

~

The fervour of Libby's kiss took every breath of air from Robert's lungs, and it took every ounce of his will to push her away. But push her away he must.

"Say you care about me," he said, his voice ragged. "Say that you have feelings for me too. Or is your kiss a lie?"

It took a moment for Libby's eyes to focus, but when she turned to look at him he saw the pain that swam behind her tears. "I care," she admitted. "But I cannot marry you. I need to marry a lord."

Robert's chest constricted. "Help me to understand. What can a lord give you that I cannot? Will he love you as much as I? Will he make you *feel* the way I do?"

"He will give me what I need. Security.

Safety." Libby spoke so quietly he almost missed her words.

Shaking his head, Robert opened his palms. "But I would never let anything happen to you. Surely you believe that?"

Her mouth turned down. "But you cannot offer the thick walls and strong defences of a castle."

"I can offer you a house in Paris. Why do you feel the need of a castle?"

Libby swallowed, then sat down on Flam's bed and patted the space beside her. "If I tell you, you must never tell anyone else. I only tell you so that you will understand why we cannot marry." She took a deep breath. "One night last year when my stepfather was away, English reivers attacked Preston Tower. But they didn't just take our cattle. They took a hostage."

His heart sinking, Robert took her hands. "You?"

"Aye."

Black clouds dimmed Robert's vision. "Did they harm you?"

~

Libby didn't answer for a moment, as memories crowded in, threatening to overcome the slim hold she had on her emotions. Then she gave the tiniest of nods. "One of the reivers, Black Jack Heron, had me on the front of his horse. He smelled disgusting, and he did not keep his hands to himself…"

"What did he do to you?" Robert growled.

"He…" *I cannot tell him what happened. For he would surely hate and despise me if he knew.* "He wanted to ransom me. For gold." Robert's grip on her hands tightened. "But Lord Home and his men followed our tracks, and caught up with us at Etal. Black Jack was captured, and his band wiped out." A shiver ran down her spine. "So, you see, if word got out, my reputation would be ruined."

She looked up at him. "And that is why I need to marry an influential lord, before any rumours from England reach the ears of the Scottish nobility and ruin my chances. I need a strong Lord who could quash any scandal and keep me safe from retribution by the Heron clan."

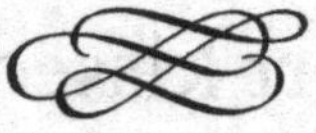

CHAPTER 22

THERE IS SOMETHING *she isn't telling me,* thought Robert. *For I have seen how quickly gossip spreads from England to Scotland. If the story was told anywhere, 'twould already be known here. But if she will not tell me, I cannot pry further.* Robert lifted her fingers to his lips and kissed her hands. "My lady, your secret is safe with me."

It matters not what her secret is—I love her anyway. I just have to convince her that a lord is not what she needs. He stood, and pulled her to her feet. "Now, we should sleep. Call one of the other ladies to watch over Mary, and I will away to the Carter's Rest. But first," he pulled her closer, "let me bid you goodnight."

Tenderly, Robert kissed Libby; a kiss that spoke of yearning, adoration and desire; a kiss that made his heart pound and caused her breath to race; a kiss that hinted at more —so much more. "Promise me one thing," he whispered, his voice thick with emotion.

Libby's blue eyes were dark with longing, her lips parted and her chest heaving. She didn't speak, merely inclined her head.

"Promise me that you will not marry unless you find a lord who will love you as well as I," he touched a finger to her lips, "and kiss you as well as I."

An unfair request, for few men have been schooled in love by ladies whose life's work is pleasure and coquetry. But I need every advantage to win this maid. "For you deserve the best, my love."

~

Libby smoothed the front of her dress, playing for time to allow her pulse to slow and her cheeks to cool.

This night had not gone as she expected, and Robert had been a revelation, even if he had tempted her to abandon her plan. "Yes, I want the best," she answered slowly. *But I also want a castle and a title,* added her traitorous thoughts.

She picked up a candle, and quashed the flutter of guilt that she could not give him the answer he wanted. "I will go waken Flam —she is on the spare cot in my room. You should rest, and I am so tired I can hardly keep my eyes open."

Nodding, Robert turned to his valise and began tidying his medicines. When Libby reappeared a couple of minutes later with Mary Fleming, he stood ready at the door.

Flam took one look at the queen and

turned to Robert; her face wreathed in smiles. "Monsieur Nau, you have worked wonders!"

Robert lifted a shoulder. "'Tis nothing. I am only glad to have helped." He opened a hand to acknowledge Libby. "And I was assisted by Lady Preston. I could not have done it on my own."

"Well, you should go and sleep now. I will watch over the queen." With a tilt of her head, Flam caught Libby's eye. "Lady Preston will see you out and check that the tower door is locked behind you."

But the guards will do that, thought Libby, and quirked her brow at Flam.

Flam just waved her fingers daintily, encouraging them to leave.

Shadows danced around them like forbidding black giants as they padded silently down the spiral staircase. While they were still out of earshot of the guards, Robert halted. "Will you walk by the river in the morning?" he asked, his voice low.

Libby pursed her lips. "I had not thought past tonight. Mayhap."

"You should." Robert's smile made her heart flip like a river otter playing in a clear-water eddy. "Doctor's orders."

CHAPTER 23

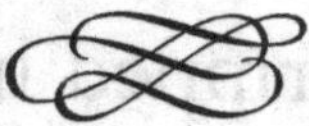

SATURDAY 26TH OCTOBER

THE FIRST PART of his morning run passed in something of a stupor as Robert fought off the tiredness that hung around him like a cloud.

Unsurprisingly, after the events and declarations of last night, he had hardly slept. But the bracing air and the blood-pumping exercise did its job, and by the time he reached the part of the riverbank where he usually met Libby his mind was clear and his spirits high in anticipation of talking with her once more.

But the footpath was empty.

Robert's steps slowed, and he spun in a circle, scanning the area. *There is no sign of her. Why would she not come?* *Have I scared her?* An icy hand gripped his heart. *Was it too much, to declare my love for her?* But she had seemed to care too—had *said* she cared. Could she have changed her mind?

Perhaps in the cold light of day she had thought better of meeting him. *Or perhaps she has decided 'tis better not to encourage a poor doctor like me.* His shoulders drooped. *That will be it. She seeks a rich lord, after all.*

Turning away from the town, he headed north, seeking solace in the repetitive movement of running, and oblivion in the pain of cramped and burning muscles.

"Libby." Someone was shaking her shoulders. "Libby! Wake up! The queen is sick again!"

Her knuckles rubbing bleary eyes, Libby blinked at Ebba Seton. "But... but she was fine last night." *Has the poisoner struck again?*

In a trice, Libby had thrown off the bedcovers, splashed water on her face, fastened a blue kirtle over her cambric chemise, and stuffed her feet into a pair of velvet slippers.

While Libby dressed, Ebba explained the situation. "Mary woke early this morning, while it was still dark, and Flam gave her some wine. But very soon after that, she swooned again, and she is so cold and stiff I fear for her life."

"We should send for Monsieur Nau. He healed her last night when she was cold."

Ebba lifted a shoulder and stepped towards the door. "We already sent a page to get him. But he is not at his lodgings." Her face grey and lined with worry, she motioned for Libby to follow her. "We hoped that you might know where to find him."

Hurrying down the stairs behind Ebba, Libby saw from the weak sunlight filtering through the tiny leaded windows that it was past dawn. *I overslept. He will be wondering where I am.* "He usually goes running at this time of day. Get the page to check the path by the river."

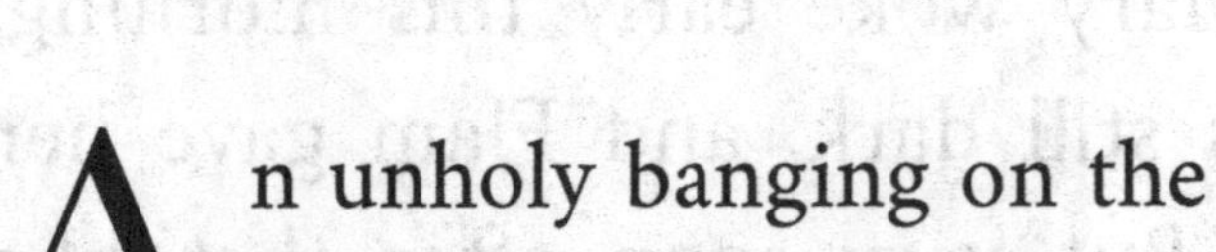

An unholy banging on the oak door of his chamber roused Bothwell from dreams of glory and had him reaching for his sword before his eyes were even fully open. "Paris," he shouted angrily, "find out who interrupts my slumber and risks my wrath."

Flinging open the door, Paris met the intruder with the point of his sword. "Who disturbs my lord's sleep?"

The hostile welcome silenced their visitor, a fair-haired lad whose face had turned a similar colour to his green hose.

Paris lowered his sword and raised his eyebrows. "'Tis the queen's page."

"Speak, boy." Bothwell swung his legs out of the bed with a grunt. "It had better be urgent."

"Forgive me, my lords." The page bowed low, suddenly remembering his manners. "'Tis the queen. She has fallen ill again and they seek the French doctor." He gazed wide-eyed around the room, as if expecting Nau to jump from behind a drape or crawl from under the bed. "They wondered if you might know his whereabouts."

"Have you tried the Carter's Rest?"

The page nodded. "He is not there."

By this time Bothwell had pulled on his doublet and thrown a baldrick over his shoulder. He pointed at his manservant. "Paris, go rouse my captain and get him to take ten of our men and scour the town for the doctor. Tell them to check the brothels and the ale-houses. If they find Nau, they are to escort him to Hartrigge House with all haste."

Paris nodded and made for the door.

"Paris!" Bothwell called him back. "Meet me at the queen's house. I will get the boy to help me walk over. But if my men have not found Nau by mid-morning, tell them to report to me back here. For I am due another treatment and the Frenchman is not usually late."

When Libby entered the queen's bedchamber and saw Mary motionless on the bed once more, her courage failed. "She—she's so pale."

Flam waved them in. "Yes. But she was ill yesterday and you healed her. You and the doctor. You must try again."

"I cannot—not on my own."

Ebba clasped her shoulder. "You must try. Until we can find the doctor, you are her best hope."

"Doctor? Who speaks of me?" said a voice behind them.

Libby's jaw dropped. For 'twas not Robert, but Monsieur Lusgerie, his white hair plastered damply to his scalp and a small leather case tucked under his arm.

Flam was the first to recover her manners. "Monsieur Lusgerie! Good morning. We were—"

"I heard the queen was ill again." Lusgerie bustled forward, waving Libby and Ebba out of his way, and motioning imperiously for Flam to give him her seat. "Let me examine Her Grace."

The ladies exchanged a look, but there was little they could do. For Lusgerie was the queen's physician, and a physician was what she needed.

Clutching the enamelled crucifix she wore around her neck like a talisman, Ebba addressed the doctor. "Monsieur, if there is anything you need, just say the word and we will fetch it for you."

Lusgerie looked up at them, his nose glowing red even at this early hour. He looked at each lady in turn and then settled on Libby. "You! Stay here in case I need help. The rest of you," he made a flicking motion with his wrist, "give us some space."

Libby looked from Ebba to Flam, her eyes wide. "I'll do what I can," she whispered. "But see if you can find Robert."

At Libby's use of Robert's first name, Flam raised an eyebrow, but thankfully she said nothing.

Ebba gave a curt nod. "We will do our utmost. And we will pray for the queen's soul."

CHAPTER 24

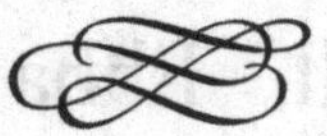

B Y THE TIME Bothwell arrived at Hartrigge house, it was a hive of activity and a hotbed of gossip. Grey-haired men in sombre doublets stood in knots muttering in low voices; servants scurried up and down stairs with jugs of ale or bowls of porridge; and the Maries sat whispering around the fire in the banqueting hall, their faces pale and their hands fluttering.

Bothwell glared at the fair-haired page. "Stay here," he hissed, and squared his shoulders before walking across to the ladies with as proud a stride as he could manage. "Good morrow," he said with a bow, addressing himself to Mary Seton. "What news of the queen?"

"Lord Bothwell." Ebba gave him a nod. "The doctor is with her now."

"Ah!" Bothwell's face creased into a smile. "They found the Frenchman!"

Ebba shook her head. "Not Monsieur Nau. Monsieur Lusgerie."

Bothwell balled his hands into fists, clenching his jaw so that he would not curse in front of the ladies. "That ne'er-do-well! He is more like to kill her than heal her." He jerked his chin at Ebba. "Take me to the queen."

~

With Lusgerie busy beside the queen, muttering and tutting under his breath as he examined her, Libby moved around the bottom of the bed and onto Flam's cot, where she had sat last night.

But when she picked up Mary's right hand, Libby almost dropped it in shock. *She is so cold! And stiff!* Libby's spirits quailed at the enormity of the task she faced. For Mary seemed even worse than she had last night when it had taken two of them more than four hours to restore her to health.

Gritting her teeth, Libby pushed her worry aside and began to rub and massage the queen's skin as she had been taught by Robert. There was no stimulant cream, but the friction of Libby's touch should generate at least a little heat. *If only Robert were here. I cannot do this on my own.*

She had worked on the queen for only a minute when Lusgerie's mumbling ceased and he turned his beady eyes on her. "What are you doing?" he demanded, alcohol fumes lacing his breath.

"Trying to warm the queen."

Lusgerie waggled his fingers dismissively. "You waste your time. Get a servant to bank the fire. That will do more good."

"But—"

"Do as I say!" Lusgerie roared, and Libby dropped the queen's hand in shock.

Rebelliously, she tucked Mary's arm under the bedcovers before scuttling out of the room to find a housemaid.

On her way downstairs, Libby almost bumped into Lord Bothwell and Mary Seton who were ascending slowly, his hand on her arm and his steps laborious.

Ebba's brows pinched together. "Libby! I thought you were with Lusgerie and the queen?"

"I was. I was trying to help her, like Monsieur Nau showed me last night." Libby lifted a shoulder. "But he stopped me and sent me to get the fire attended to."

Bothwell's expression darkened. "We cannot leave him alone with the queen." He gave Libby a significant look. "He may be in league with the poisoner."

Libby gasped. "I—I must..." But she didn't finish the sentence, or the thought. Instead, she spun around, raced back up the stairs and burst into the queen's room. "Monsieur!"

Lusgerie's back was to the door, as he rummaged in his black case. He whirled round, his face thunderous. "What is the meaning of this?"

Thinking quickly, Libby gestured at the stairwell. "The earl of Bothwell comes to visit the queen."

A moment later, Ebba and Bothwell reached the small landing outside Mary's room. "Good morrow, Monsieur Lusgerie," Bothwell said stiffly.

"My lord." Lusgerie gave a perfunctory bow, then swept an arm at the queen. "As you can see, Her Grace is seriously ill."

"So I see." Lowering his voice, Bothwell

addressed Libby. "Since you are friendly with Nau, it might be best if you go look for him." Jerking his chin at the old doctor, Bothwell added ambiguously, "Lady Seton and I will keep watch here."

The pain in Robert's heart drove him miles along the banks of the Jed Water, and he had reached Walkersknowe before reason asserted itself and he turned back towards Jedburgh.

His pace slowed to a jog, his feet aching and a blister burning his right heel with every step he took. But an idea was forming. *I have gold now, from the queen. I will see if it will buy me a small house in Edinburgh, and in the evenings, when the ambassador does not need me, I will see patients, and earn more gold. If I live frugally, I should soon have enough to buy a house in Paris. Mayhap then Libby will consider me.*

It was not the best of plans, for he had no title and could not compete with the likes of Hugh Somerville. But at least he had a target, which was better than living aimlessly. And he had a little hope, to give his life direction.

He had almost reached Jedburgh when a small pool caught his eye. Carved by the river currents under the mangled roots of a juniper tree, the water looked clear and inviting—and just the thing to soothe his sore heel.

The temptation was too much. A moment later, Robert had sat on the hard-packed dirt of the river bank, pulled off his boots and short hose, and dangled his feet in the water.

Bliss.

Leaning back on his elbows, he closed his eyes and raised his face to the warmth of the sun, emptying his mind of everything save the ripple of the river and the murmuring eddies that swirled past his feet.

He sat there for fully five minutes, the freshness of the river cooling his skin and soothing his mood. But even as his feet revived and restored, it made the rest of him feel sticky and dirty. Looking up and downstream, he spotted no onlookers. *Shall I?* Another glance at the pool decided him. *Yes!*

In the time it took for a lazy leaf to float across the mouth of the pool, Robert's shirt and doublet had joined his boots and hose on the riverbank, leaving him wearing only his breeches. He lowered himself into the pool, breath catching as the cold made his chest contract, but his skin tingling and feeling more alive than it had for weeks.

It took a full minute for his body temperature to lower enough that he became accustomed to the chill, but once it did, he wondered how he had not done this before.

Robert took regular baths, believing that

cleanliness would ward off many illnesses, and he encouraged his patients to do so too. But this was somehow better, more natural. *I shall bathe in the river more often*, he thought, rolling onto his back and floating with his arms outstretched.

Sunlight dappled his face as it filtered through the branches of the trees above, and Robert tried to imagine what he must look like to a bird or a squirrel in the high branches. *Like Christ on the cross*, he thought, *martyred for a cause.*

The thought inspired him to pray.

A miracle, he petitioned heaven, *I need a miracle to change Libby's heart and make her come to love me as I do her. 'Tis not a selfish wish, for she could help me with the poor at my hospital, just as she helped me with the queen last night.* His heart eased a little. *Just one miracle. Please. 'Tis all I ask.*

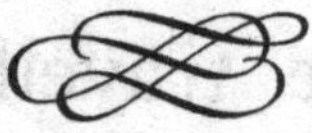

HURRYING ALONG THE path by the Jed Water, Libby's head turned this way and that, searching for Robert's tall frame and dark hair.

Bothwell's men scoured the town, knocking on doors and checking down alleyways. But Libby felt sure that Robert would be here, in the countryside, not cooped up in a tavern or gambling in some den of iniquity. *If he was in Jedburgh, they would've found him by now. So he must be out here somewhere.*

The decision to go upstream or downstream had been a difficult one, for if she got it wrong she'd be travelling further away from him with every step. But downstream was where he ran most often, and she hoped, for the queen's sake, that she'd guessed right.

Worry ate at her heart, a dead weight in her chest that grew heavier with every step that she took. Always before her was a picture of the queen's white face and still body, driving her legs to move faster and her arms to pump harder, until she was almost running, something she'd never have been fit enough to do until she started her morning walks with Robert.

If it hadn't been for the flash of his white linen shirt folded on the riverbank, Libby might have missed her target and run straight past. But the tidy pile of clothes stopped her in her tracks—and the vision that she saw in the languid waters almost stopped her heart.

His eyes closed, Robert floated in the river with his arms outstretched like some ancient martyr. However, that was where the resemblance to a religious icon stopped. For he was naked apart from his black breeches, which clung to every ridge and valley of his slim hips and well-toned legs, leaving little to the imagination.

But it was his bare chest which drew Libby's attention—and had her thinking that she would need to pray to the saints for forgiveness every day for the next month. Improper thoughts flashed through her mind, sending her pulse racing even as her eyes were glued to his body.

Teasing curls of dark hair led the eye from the powerful, flat planes of Robert's shoulders, down his wide chest, and across a stomach that rippled with lean muscle. It was a vision made in heaven—a vision that ended with a tantalising trail of darkness that disappeared into the top of his breeches.

Blinking hard, Libby dragged her mind back to her urgent mission, and cleared her throat. "Ah, Monsieur Nau!"

Robert's eyes flew open, his expression somewhere between shock and gratitude. "Lady Preston!"

Bringing his legs underneath him, he stood, unselfconsciously, and wiped the river water from his eyes.

Transfixed once more, Libby fought the desire to stretch out a finger and follow the trickles of water that ran down his chest. She swallowed. "Monsieur Nau, the queen is sick again. Worse this time. And Lusgerie attends her. They sent me to fetch you."

Robert's eyes widened, and he stepped towards the river bank, the muscles of his arms bunching and cording as he levered himself out of the water. Quickly, he pulled on his boots, pushed his arms into his shirt and grabbed his doublet. "Can you run?" he asked.

"I'll try," Libby replied, hoping that her pulse had recovered sufficiently from the sight of his handsome body that her heart would not give out.

"Come," he said, took her hand, and set off at a jog towards the town.

To Bothwell's mind, Lusgerie did little to help the queen. He bustled about, mumbling incoherently and stopping every now and again to shake his head and suck air through his teeth.

But he made no effort to warm her, other than allowing the servants to bank the fire and Ebba to pile extra blankets on top of Mary's bedcovers.

Lying inert on her narrow bed the queen was ice-cold; her face white and her eyes closed. She looked worse than she had last night. Much worse.

Bothwell feared for her life. *Is it Moray's scheming that has caused this? Could it be poison again?* Eyeing the doctor, Bothwell debated whether to confront him. But he had no proof that Lusgerie was in cahoots with the bastard, just a hunch. 'Twould *be better to bide my time and gather facts.*

As a man of action, this inactivity clawed at his throat and had him pacing from door to window, limping and hobbling worse than a sheep destined for the butcher. *But I must stay. I must keep the queen safe from poison until my men find the French doctor.* And it seemed like Nau was the queen's only hope now, for Lusgerie appeared to have given up.

"Send for the bishop," the doctor instructed Mary's page solemnly, "methinks her time is near." Fumbling with the latch on the nearest window, he muttered something about allowing the queen's soul to fly free.

Bothwell didn't recognise the sound that escaped from his lungs. It was as if a wild animal had been cornered, growling, snarling and bellowing its frustration. His eyes stinging, he stomped across the room and thumped down onto the spare cot.

Compared to his square palms and squat fingers, the queen's hand looked like a delicate leaf, rimed in hoar frost and so brittle that it might break in two. Tenderly, he covered Mary's hand with both of his, and raised it to his chest, dropping his head so that his lips touched the ends of her fingers.

Beside him, Ebba moaned in distress and fell to her knees in prayer, elbows on Mary's bed and her lips moving silently as tears tracked unheeded down her cheeks.

She has the right of it, Bothwell thought, and wished he too could pray. For Mary's life was slipping away, and it would need a miracle to save her.

His boots clattering on the stairs of Hartrigge House, Robert's spirits quailed. Servants tiptoed by with their eyes downcast, and, through the doorway of the banqueting hall he caught a glimpse of Flam and Beth, huddled together and weeping profusely.

"Prepare yourself," he murmured to Libby as they burst into the queen's chamber.

"Monsieur Nau!" The earl of Bothwell sprang to his feet, relief washing over his face. "The queen needs you, she—"

"She is gone," interrupted Lusgerie, his eyes narrowing. "So we have no need of *you*." He jabbed a finger at Robert's chest to emphasise the point.

"Quite so," said the earl, pushing his way between them and squaring his shoulders. "With the queen gone, she has no more need of her physician. So, Monsieur Lusgerie, you are released!"

"But—"

Bothwell's face was turning puce. "Do not argue, Lusgerie, just *go!*" He practically bellowed this last word, and Lusgerie visibly shrank, his ears disappearing into the collar of his shirt.

Grabbing his black case, the old doctor scuttled out of the room and down the stairs.

"Monsieur Nau, your patient." Bothwell ushered him towards the bed.

For a moment, Robert worried that he'd been brought here as a stooge, to be blamed for the death of the queen, and vilified—or worse—when he failed to save her life. But Bothwell's next words eased Robert's mind somewhat.

"You are our only hope, doctor, for you healed my wound," he touched his side, "and your medicines have revived Her Grace more than once. I can only hope that you might be successful again."

"As do I," Robert replied, casting his eyes over Mary's prone form. He touched her arm. *Freezing.* "Close the windows!" he commanded, sitting by her bed. "And stoke the fire!"

Ebba hurried off to find a housemaid, and Robert motioned for Libby to sit at the other side, as she had last night. "I'll need my valise," he threw over his shoulder as an afterthought, "if you could send someone for it."

"I took the liberty of fetching it already." Bothwell limped to the door and shouted down the stairwell. "Paris!"

But Robert hardly heard the commotion as he focussed on the queen, his heart sinking as he assessed her condition. Mary did, indeed, appear lifeless, her skin chilled and heartbeat undetectable. *But I must be sure.* 'Twould *be unforgivable to make a mistake of this import.*

Holding his right cheek over Mary's mouth so that he might feel even the faintest breath, Robert turned his head and concentrated on determining whether her chest rose and fell, by even the tiniest amount. Opposite him, Libby had hold of the queen's right arm, rubbing and manipulating the flesh as they'd done the previous night.

"Get the salve," he muttered, when Paris appeared carrying Robert's valise.

A full minute passed while Robert stared fixedly at Mary's chest, willing it to move.

At the other side of the bed, Libby began to massage liniment into Mary's hand, then smoothed it past her wrist and up her arm. "She is so cold," Libby whispered, "and stiff."

The astringent aroma made Robert's eyes sting, and he sat up with a grimace, his heart breaking. For he saw no sign that the queen was breathing. *Mayhap Lusgerie was right.* Shoulders wound tight as a bow-string, he lifted a hand to stop Libby's ministrations. "Lady Preston—"

Libby's gasp interrupted him. "Her arm! Feel it!" Holding Mary's arm off the covers, she pointed at the pale flesh above the queen's elbow.

Reaching across, Robert placed his palm over Mary's arm, and his eyes widened. "You are right!"

Bothwell hurried over. "What is it?"

"Her arm—'tis almost warm, compared to the rest of her, and the flesh is not stiff. There is yet hope." Robert leaned down and opened his valise. "Send Paris to the kitchens for some cloths. We need to make bandages —and lots of them!"

CHAPTER 26

BOTHWELL WATCHED IN wonderment as the Frenchman and Lady Preston bandaged the queen's limbs, starting at her big toes and winding the cloth tightly until her legs were bound to the knee and arms to the elbow.

"Lady Preston, start massaging her shoulders and arms if you please." Nau instructed when they had finished bandaging, then glanced at Bothwell. "And Lord Bothwell, if you could send for some wine. I need to administer a clyster."

"I will go myself," Bothwell replied, and set off down the stairs as quickly as his sore body would allow him.

The great hall, when he got there, was busier than when he had last been downstairs. By the fire, the Maries whispered in hushed tones about whether cloth would arrive from Edinburgh in time to make mourning clothes. A knot of lords by the middle window discussed whether the funeral should take place in Stirling or Edinburgh.

Bothwell's jaw tightened.

At the long banqueting table, Maitland sat writing a letter to the king, telling him of his wife's demise. Lord Seton and the earl of Huntly discussed how they would maintain public order when the queen's death was announced.

Bothwell's nostrils flared.

But, worst of all, near the door, Moray stacked silverware from a cabinet into the waiting arms of one of his servants, as if looting a tomb.

Bothwell stamped his foot. "She is not dead yet!" he roared, ending all conversation and turning every eye to the doorway in which he stood.

After a moment's stunned silence, Moray looked down his nose at Bothwell. "Not dead?" he said with a sneer. "Why then did the doctor send for a priest?"

Bothwell spoke through gritted teeth. "Because the doctor is an incompetent fool who consorts with the queen's enemies rather than listening to the one who pays him."

There was a shocked hush, broken after a few seconds by Mary Seton's thin voice. "What then should we do?"

"Hope," said Bothwell, locking eyes with each one of them in turn, from left to right around the room, "and pray." He drew himself to his full height. "For without the queen, this country will be in the hands of Lord Darnley…" The last person Bothwell's gaze alighted on was Moray, and he tilted his chin defiantly. "Or worse."

~

At some of the harsh treatments they administered to the poor queen, Libby almost found herself in tears. Working like demons to restore some warmth and life to her limbs, Libby rubbed Mary's shoulders and arms while Robert manipulated her legs.

They massaged and pummelled her for hours, until her colour and breathing improved and her skin became merely cool, rather than frigid. Next, Robert moved to her stomach, circling more gently with his fingertips and pressing with the heel of his hand. After about twenty minutes of this, Robert looked up. "'Tis time to administer an enema," he pronounced, and rummaged in his valise.

Libby could hardly watch this next part of the queen's treatment, but a short time later it produced results—results that had Robert's handsome face distorted into a scowl.

"Did it not work?" Libby asked.

Robert wrinkled his nose. "It worked. It worked well. But the evacuations are…" he paused, as if searching for the right word, "suspicious."

These robust therapies began to show an improvement, however, and the queen gradually warmed; moaning if they worked too vigorously on her abdomen. After another hour or so, Robert opened her mouth and forced her to swallow an emetic of wine and herbs, and this produced the biggest change yet.

In the corner of the room, Bothwell's face turned a shade of green as Libby held back

Mary's hair and the queen vomited quantities of corrupt blood into a bowl held by Robert.

"Bien. Get it all out," Robert said, rubbing gentle circles on her back. "'Tis better out than in."

When she'd exhausted herself, the queen sat back, her eyes closed and a sheen of sweat on her brow and upper lip.

Robert wiped her chin, then offered some wine. "To take the taste away," he said.

After a few sips, Mary lay back again, but this time she seemed more composed. The fingers of her right hand twitched on the coverlet, then crept forward till she found Libby's hand, and gave it a tiny squeeze.

"Thank you, ma'am," Libby whispered, then caught Robert's eye.

In this unguarded moment, the Frenchman's gaze was intense, long lashes framing his dark eyes, and wide lips promising exotic pleasures. It took her breath away.

After the intensity of the few last hours treating the queen, Robert should have felt exhausted. But somehow, that brief glance from Libby energised him, for it told him that she *did* still care for him, and gave him hope that his plan might yet work. *Patience.*

"Come," he said, pulling at the cloth wrapped around Mary's feet. "Let us remove the bandages, then we can massage some life back into her arms and legs."

It took another hour, but when the queen's eyes flickered open and her mouth creased into a slow smile, Robert held out a hand. "Lady Preston, I think we can stop now."

"Oui." Mary's voice cracked, and she licked her lips, green eyes resting first on Libby, then Robert. "Merci. Merci bien."

Bothwell cleared his throat and stood, elbows tucked into his sides and hands grasping the edges of his gown. "Monsieur Nau, you have delivered us a miracle. For the queen was dead, and you have brought her back to life." He inclined his head. "I thank you. And all of Scotland thanks you!"

A miracle!

Bothwell's words reverberated around Robert's head like an echo in a cathedral.

I prayed for a miracle. He stared across at Libby, feeling guilty about the twinge of disappointment in his chest. *This was just not the miracle I imagined.*

CHAPTER 27

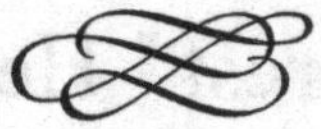

SUNDAY 27TH OCTOBER

PROPPED ON FEATHER pillows, Mary beamed at her visitors and opened a welcoming arm. "Lady Preston! Monsieur Nau! Please, come in. Are you fully recovered?"

"'Tis we who should be asking that of you, ma'am." The good-looking Frenchman bowed deeply.

"But I 'ear you worked on me all night and then all day with your healing herbs and —" she made a face, "concoctions. 'Ave you slept?"

"Yes ma'am." Nau's brow creased. "But 'tis only a day since we brought you back from the brink of death. You will take some time to recover. I hope you are not receiving visitors? You need to rest." He glanced across at Libby, the ghost of a smile playing on his lips. "Doctor's orders."

Mary inclined her head. "You are my only visitors today, apart from my Maries, who watch over me and attend to my every need, and Lord Bothwell," she fluttered a hand at the earl who stood silently in the corner by the fire, "who protects me." Her face clouded. "For I 'ear you suspect poison?"

"Unfortunately," the doctor confirmed. "The emanations from your sickness were… suspicious."

Mary was silent for a moment, picking at the edge of her sheet. *So Bothwell was right. I cannot trust my own brother.* Then she looked up, her expression resolute. "Monsieur Nau, I owe you more than I can possibly express.

Without you, without your treatments, I…" her hands clenched involuntarily, "without you, my son would have lost his mother, and our country would be reigned by a man who, it pains me to say, is most unworthy of such an honour." Lifting her chin, she looked the Frenchman in the eye. "I cannot thank you enough."

Nau bowed, dark hair flopping over his face. "'Twas an honour to be able to help."

"And I mean to 'onour you." She glanced at Bothwell. "But first, my lord Bothwell has something to say."

Bothwell took a step forward. "Monsieur Nau, you have healed my queen, and you also healed me from a grievous wound. For that, I am indebted to you." He handed Nau a rolled parchment. "'Tis the title of Elshanford Tower, near Haddington."

From where she stood next to the window, Libby's eyes widened.

Inclining his head, Bothwell added, "I

give it to you in recognition of your skill as a physician, and perseverance as a healer."

Nau looked stunned. "But—"

Mary held up a hand, silencing him. Then she motioned to Bothwell. "My lord, your sword, if you please."

Libby looked from Nau to the queen, her mouth open, as if she guessed what was coming next.

Good, thought Mary. *I needed her to hear this.*

For the queen had not been insensible the whole time Libby and the doctor worked on her, and she had heard some of what had passed between them. Ever the romantic, Mary was pleased that the events of the last days—dangerous as they had been for her— might work to the favour of the French doctor, who seemed honourable and brave, not to mention strikingly handsome.

"I cannot thank you enough," she continued, motioning for Nau to kneel before her.

"But I *can* show you my gratitude by making you a Lord of Parliament." She touched his right shoulder with the flat of the sword. "Robert Nau, physician of Paris, for works of skill and perseverance, and for saving the life of the Scots queen, I, Mary, Queen of Scots, dub thee viscount," she moved the sword to his left shoulder, "in the name of God and in the presence of these witnesses. Arise, Lord Elshanford."

Nau raised his eyes to her face, visibly moved. "Ma'am, I do not deserve such an honour. Truly. I was only doing what any physician would have done."

"And yet," Mary raised her eyebrows, "my own physician 'ad already given me up for dead, when you worked your miracles." She motioned for him to rise, then placed the sword on the bed beside her. "Also, if you agree, I will speak to the ambassador about securing your services for the royal 'ousehold. I wish you to work for me." She gave

Libby a sideways look. "And there will be an 'ouse in Edinburgh for you, too."

The Frenchman looked conflicted. "But—forgive me, ma'am, you honour me greatly. But I would not want to let the ambassador down. He relies on my medicines to help him with his condition."

Mary clenched her teeth and thought for a moment. *'Tis good to see that the doctor is loyal, even if it makes things more difficult for me.* "Let me speak with du Croc. I will see if we can come to some arrangement. Now," she held out Bothwell's sword for him to take it, "you look like you need a restorative brandy. Lord Bothwell will take you downstairs," she glanced across at Libby, "I wish to speak with Lady Preston."

Libby watched Bothwell and Robert depart from the chamber, panic rising in her chest as if her anchor disappeared below the waves. *What can the queen want with me?*

Nervously, she began to tidy the hairbrushes and goblets atop the dresser, bringing order to disorder and calming her agitation in the only way she knew how.

"My dear," the queen pointed at the chair beside her bed, "come sit with me."

Smoothing her green damask gown, Libby sat on the wooden seat, knotted her fingers together, and held her breath.

"I understand that you were also instrumental in my recovery," Mary began, "and that I have you to thank almost as much as the doctor. I am told," her lips twitched, "that you were the one to find 'im when 'e was off exploring our countryside like Christopher Columbus."

"'Twas nothing, ma'am," Libby whispered, an image of Robert's naked chest appearing, unbidden, in her mind's eye. She cleared her throat.

"Nevertheless," Mary sat forward, "I am grateful. Now," she pointed at the window-sill, "bring me my jewellery box, if you please."

Libby remembered the last time that she'd seen the briarwood casket, and protested, even as she handed it over, "I have no need of gold, Your Grace."

"Then that is just as well," Mary replied, turning the brass key and opening the lid. She lifted the lid and rummaged through the contents of the box for a few moments. "Aha! Here it is." Proudly, she displayed a bright blue sapphire ring. Holding it beside Libby's cheek, she nodded in satisfaction. "Parfait! The blue brings out the colour of your eyes. Here," she placed the ring in Libby's palm and closed her fingers over it. "Something to remember me by. And it will be perfect with that lovely blue gown you wore at the ambassador's reception."

Libby stared at the twinkling gem, her mind whirling. *I cannot refuse, for 'twould be ungrateful.* "I—I thank you ma'am. You are too kind." She rose to go and dropped a curtsey. "I shall send Flam to sit with you."

"Wait!" Mary motioned her back into the seat. "I am not finished. I wanted to talk with you before I get too tired. And before 'tis too late."

Slipping the ring into the concealed pocket in her gown, Libby lowered herself back into the chair.

"I 'ave something to share with you," Mary began, "that I hope I can trust you to keep confidential, just between the two of us."

Libby nodded, her eyes widening. *What secret could the queen possibly have to share with me?* Her heart stopped. *Or could she somehow know my secret?* Panic rose in Libby's chest.

Something of her alarm must have showed on her face because Mary placed a hand over hers. "'Tis nothing to worry about, I just wanted to tell you a story." She lay back against her pillows. "Some years ago, when I was newly widowed, and arrived in Scotland from France, my councillors were determined that I should marry. The English queen also wished for me to be wed, even though she shows no sign herself of espousing matrimony... But I digress." She reached for a silver goblet on her side-table and took a sip of wine.

"My lords proposed this suitor, and that —all Protestants of course. And Elizabeth suggested her favourite, Lord Dudley." She sniffed. "Another Protestant. But I, I was smitten by a man with dashing good looks and the lightest of feet on the dance floor. I had met him a mere handful of times, and hardly knew him. But I was determined he was the one for me." She turned a keen eye on Libby. "You know of whom I speak?"

Libby looked up from under her eyebrows. "Lord Darnley?"

"Oui. If only I had taken the time to get to know him better. For I soon discovered that a handsome face or a noble title does not mean that a man will make a good husband." Mary took another sip of her drink. "Money and titles are no guarantee of happiness, sad to say." She eyed Libby speculatively over the rim of her goblet.

"But a man who loves you for yourself, who will be honest with you, treat you like a princess and look after you till his dying day, *that* is a man worth marrying." The queen looked down at her hands, her voice quieter as she added, "I wish I had known that a long time ago."

They sat in silence for a moment, Libby's mind whirling as she tried to understand the queen's words. "Thank you, ma'am."

Mary nodded, then set the wine back on her side table. "Now, I must sleep, and you should too. Think on my words. But keep them to yourself," she cautioned.

"I will. Thank you, ma'am."

CHAPTER 28

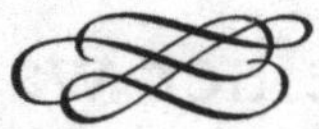

MONDAY 28TH OCTOBER

LIBBY ROSE AT dawn, her body tired after a sleepless night, but her heart light. She almost skipped down the stone stairs of Hartrigge House, wishing the guards a 'good morrow' as she slipped out of the door and headed for the riverbank.

A fine drizzle made everything grey and featureless, droplets pattering from the trees she passed, and the peaty odour of damp earth getting stronger with every step she took.

305

What if he does not come? Hurrying the last few yards, Libby dropped the hood of her woollen cloak and scanned up and down the river. 'Tis *so foggy, I cannot see.* All she could think was to make her way downstream towards their usual meeting place, so she set off northwards.

It was Robert's footsteps that first alerted her to his presence, and a moment later he almost barrelled into her, striding round a bend in the path with his arms pumping and his head high. "Lady Preston!" he said in surprise as he skidded to a halt.

"Please," she said, "call me Libby."

Robert's eyes flared. "I did not expect to see you this morning. How is the queen?"

"She passed a quiet night, I believe. Thanks to your ministrations."

He inclined his head. "And those of my able assistant."

Libby looked at her hands. "But I never

got to congratulate you last night, Lord Elshanford."

His lips twitching, he waved a hand. "Please, call me Robert."

"Doctor's orders?" she asked with a grin, and suddenly everything was back to normal between them.

"Oui," he said, and hooked her arm through his.

"Wait!" Fishing in her pocket, Libby produced the sapphire ring. "The queen gave me this last night." She looked up at him, her heart racing. "And I wanted to give it to you." Carefully, she placed it in his palm, adding, "For you said you had no ring."

Robert looked from the ring to Libby's face, his brow puckered and his lips parted. "I... had no ring," he repeated slowly, and then his face cleared. "Ah! You mean..." Then he frowned. "But you did not want me, before, when I was just a doctor. You are only interested because I am now a lord!" Shoving the ring back at her, he turned angrily and stomped away.

"No!" Libby raced after him and grabbed his arm, spinning him round. "You must understand. 'Twas the queen. She made me see. She talked about how unhappy she is with Darnley and told me that money and titles mean nothing compared to the love of a good man. And I thought about it all night, and I realised that a man who loves me with all his heart—a man *I* can love with all my heart, *that* is what's important." She searched his eyes. "For I *do* love you Robert, and I'm sorry that I was too foolish to realise, until now. But," she stared at the ring in her hand, "I wanted you to know the truth."

∼

*T*ruth, thought Robert, and swallowed. "If we are talking truth, then there is something I must tell you, before you say any more, or make a decision you might regret."

Libby shook her head. "I will not—"

Putting a finger to her lips, Robert shook his head. "Wait until you hear my story." Taking her arm, he led her slowly back towards the town. "You know I am from Paris," he started. "And I studied there to become a doctor. But schooling in France is not free. My brother, Claude, he paid my university fees from his earnings as a lawyer."

"Your brother is a lawyer!" Libby exclaimed, her eyebrows raised. "You never said."

"Oui. But it was also expensive for him to go to school. My mother paid his fees, before she died, God rest her soul."

"Oh, I'm so sorry. I didn't know that you'd lost your mother."

Robert lifted a shoulder and looked sideways at her. "Our mother was the one who made all this possible, from the money she made running her… business."

"Her business," Libby repeated, her voice faltering.

"Oui. She ran a house for ladies who… tended to the needs of the gentlemen of the city."

Libby's jaw dropped. "You mean…"

"A brothel," Robert declared, and turned her to face him. "But it was my mother's business that made me the man I am, and allowed me to qualify as a physician, rather than living a life of poverty in the slums of Paris. So I thank God for her, every day of my life."

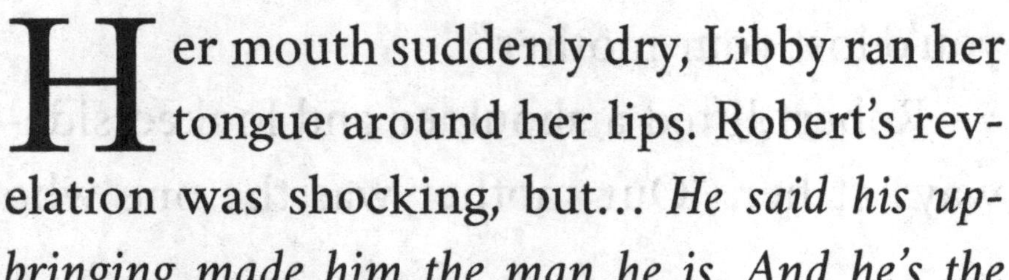

Her mouth suddenly dry, Libby ran her tongue around her lips. Robert's revelation was shocking, but… *He said his upbringing made him the man he is. And he's the*

most wonderful, thoughtful and clever man I've ever met. Should I hold his upbringing against him?

"And that is my secret," Robert concluded, letting out a deep breath. Tension showed in the muscles of his jaw. "So I will understand if you want nothing more to do with me."

Secret.

Libby's heart pounded. *Dare I tell him my secret?* But what had the queen said about honesty being important? She mustered all her courage and looked him in the eye.

"On the contrary," Libby said, "'Twas your upbringing that made you the man you are. The man I love."

Robert's shoulders sagged as the tension left his body.

"But I have a secret too, which I cannot hide from you any longer." She clenched her fist, the ring she held biting into her palm, the pain helping to focus her thoughts. "I told you about the reivers, and Black Jack?"

Robert nodded.

"Well, Black Jack did not just kidnap me. Before he was captured, he… forced himself on me." Unbidden, the memory of his blackened teeth and the stench of his rotten breath rolled over her, and she screwed her eyes shut, clenching her fist even harder. "So, you see, I am ruined, and no man who knows the truth will want me."

A finger under her chin lifted her face, and soft lips gently touched her mouth. "This man wants you," Robert breathed.

Libby's eyes flew open. "But—"

Robert silenced her with another kiss. "I am not a virgin either. But no man ever lets that worry them. Why should it be different for a woman?" He prized open her hand and took the ring from her fingers. "And you were forced against your will. 'Twas hardly your fault."

Dropping to one knee, he ignored the muddy ground and the rain that fell from the sky. Instead, he opened his arms wide. "Libby Logan," he declared, "if you will have me as your husband, I vow to show you the ways of love, to show you the joy there is to be had when a man beds a woman with only her pleasure in mind, and to show you the heights of bliss that are to be found when two people leave their inhibitions behind, and become as one. If you will let me, I will love you, cherish you, and adore you, till death us do part."

For a moment, Libby was speechless, a tide of happiness welling inside her as her future, once so unclear, rolled out before her like a map. *Robert. Paris. Helping at the hospital. Mayhap even some little boys who look like Robert if the Lord wills it.* Then her mouth twitched. "Is that what the doctor orders?"

Robert nodded, his face breaking out into a wide grin. "Doctor's orders."

EPILOGUE

SATURDAY 9TH NOVEMBER 1566

Bothwell applied his spurs to the flanks of his grey cob, urging it to keep up with the long legs of the queen's palfrey. Trotting behind them, the lords and ladies of the Scottish court fanned out across the moorland like a colourful carpet.

Ahead—and at the rear, for the safety of the nobility—were the ranks of soldiers, nearly a thousand in total, who were under his command as Lieutenant of the Borders.

He addressed the queen, "Your grace, is this speed acceptable to you? I can ask the men to ride slower if you wish."

"'Tis fine, Lord Bothwell. I am recovered, and heartily sick of Jedburgh, if I am honest. And we cannot dally if we want to get to Kelso before the Sabbath."

"Very well, ma'am."

"But you can help, my lord."

Bothwell's eyes widened. "I can?" Then he remembered his manners. "Anything for you, ma'am. Whatever you desire."

"Tell me of your fight with Jock Elliot. 'Twill make the journey pass more quickly. I hear he was a beast of a man."

"He was that, ma'am, as dangerous an adversary as ever there was." Bothwell proceeded to tell her of his fight with the reiver, embellishing his part, of course, to make him seem more brave and worthy, and painting Elliot as a dastardly villain. Which he undoubtedly had been.

But, as he spoke, he watched the queen's face closely. The first part of his plan to gain the crown was in place—he had healed from his wounds. The next step was to get back into favour at court—and, considering that the queen had specially requested for him to ride beside her, mayhap he could now count that part of the plan as already accomplished?

"I am glad," Mary waved a gloved hand in his direction, "that you were able to vanquish him. It seems that the Borders are more under control now. My decision to make you lieutenant was a good one."

Bothwell ducked his head. "Thank you, ma'am, you are most kind."

"And you are most brave, my lord."

Was that a hint of admiration on her countenance? His heart leapt in his chest. Could he dare to hope…

The next part of his plan would be *much*

easier if the queen were to have feelings for him. So very much easier.

"Thank you ma'am," he said again, curling his lips into an uncharacteristic smile.

Yes, he still had to find a way to divorce his dreary wife Jean, but he would find a way. By far the hardest task would be that of freeing Mary from her marriage to that sot, Darnley. But it would be *immeasurably* easier if she was favourably disposed towards him.

Even better if he could get some of the other lords to agree to his plans. Had Maitland not hinted that the queen wished to be rid of the king? *Yes. That will be my next step.* Get the agreement of the lords. Then deal with the king.

Bothwell would gain the crown. *Soon.* He was sure of it. Puffing out his chest, he lifted his chin, imagining the weight of a circlet on his head and ermine on his shoulders.

Soon.

THE END

Mary's story will continue in Book 3 of The Reivers series, **A Love Concealed**.

Read on for a sample:

AN EXCERPT FROM A LOVE CONCEALED

DECEMBER 4TH, 1566

Margaret Carwood thrust her hands on her hips, and raised her chin. "Who do you think you are, to claim the part of the king?" she demanded.

Behind her, a fire burned in the wide fireplace of the great hall of Craigmillar Castle. But the glowing logs only served to take the worst of the chill from the November air. Outside, the sky was filled with clouds the colour of steel and a merciless wind whistled up the hill from Little France, buffeting off the curtain wall and swirling around the high tower.

"Only his direct descendant, my lady," replied the laird of Fincastle, with a lift of a well-muscled shoulder. Sat on a window seat in an alcove formed by the depth of the thick stone walls, John Stewart of Tulliepowries appeared unconcerned by the great honour he was asking. "Robert the Bruce was my great-grandfather's great-grandfather. So it seems only right that I should play him."

Aye, but I'll bet The Bruce never had eyes so blue nor hair so black. Clenching her jaw, Margaret turned her back on the Highlander and addressed Sebastian Pages, who acted as master of ceremonies to Mary Queen of Scots and directed all her masques. "What say you, Bastian? Should we allow this man to take the lead part? 'Twould be his first role here at Craigmillar, and he's been here but five minutes. Quite a coup for a laird newly arrived at court!"

The Frenchman rubbed his chin. "But they are hardly queueing out the door to join us." He eyed the well-built laird with his broad chest and square jaw. "Let him audition for the part by rehearsing with us this afternoon. If he can act, good. If he cannot, then I can step in. I wrote the words, after all. But The Bruce was tall and strong, and," Bastian waved a hand at his slim figure, encased in a blue doublet and matching trunk hose, "much as I would wish to claim those attributes, I am not. Here," he thrust a sheaf of papers at the Highlander, "these are the lines." He clapped his hands. "We will rehearse the third scene." Giving Margaret a sideways look, he added, "That will let us see if he can *really* act."

Margaret's chest constricted. "But…" *Scene three is the love tryst. I would have to kiss the laird. A man I don't even know.* "I cannot—"

Waving his fingers at her, Bastian dismissed her protests. "We all know that you are a good actress, Lady Carwood. This should be easy for you. 'Tis the Highlander who will find it difficult."

I n the grey winter light that filtered through the leaded windows, John leafed through the hand-written script, his heart sinking. Scene three had The Bruce bidding farewell to his wife on the eve of Bannock-burn. With her flame-coloured hair and her heart-shaped face Lady Carwood might be beautiful, but she had a tongue on her as sharp as the edge of a broadsword and a fiery personality that matched her hair. *Not the lady I would have chosen to kiss.*

Unfolding his long legs, he stepped from the window embrasure. *But if I want to re-build our castle, I need to raise funds. And I wilna make a fortune if I dinna get my name known at court.* He clenched his jaw. *Best get it over and done with.* "I'm ready."

Bastian shepherded him to a spot at the back of the hall, at the opposite end to the great fireplace where the queen would sit to watch their masque. "You are about to lead your country to war against the English. If all goes well, you will be a hero. But if it goes badly, you will never see your wife, Elizabeth de Burgh, again." He pointed at a spot two paces to John's right. "There is your mark. And here—" he indicated a dark shadow on the flagstone floor, "is yours, Lady Carwood. You know what you have to do. With this scene, we want to make them cry."

With sadness, I presume, no' tears of laughter, John thought with a wry smile, standing at his appointed place, half-facing forward, and half towards Lady Carwood.

John took a deep breath, and focussed his mind on the woman in front of him, imagining how he'd have felt if he'd had one last chance to bid farewell to his Lizzy. Just the thought of it made his throat thicken and his chest swell. *If only I could have told her, one more time, how much she meant tae me.*

Swallowing, he took Lady Carwood's hand and started to read from the script.

"Elizabeth, dear heart, we go into battle against the English the 'morn." He kissed her hand and looked into her eyes. "Will ye wait for me?"

"Aye, and I shall pray for ye too, sire," replied Lady Carwood, taking a step closer so they were only a hands-width apart.

With the rustle of her garments came the scent of vanilla, making his nostrils flare. In the dim light from the candle sconces her green eyes gleamed like lustrous emeralds. *She really is breath-taking. 'Tis a shame she's more prickly than a hedgehog.* He cleared his throat, and dropped his eyes to the script. "Edward's army are camped to the south, and my scouts say they have twice our numbers. But we are fighting for our land, and for our freedom!" His voice dropped again, and he added some warmth to the next words. "And I will be fighting for you, my love. Give me a token of your affections that I can take into battle with me."

A slim finger rose to his cheek, and traced the line of his jaw, then drifted across to his bottom lip. "I will give you more than a token," she whispered.

For a moment, John was unable to breathe. Without checking the script for his next lines, he responded instinctively, dropping his mouth to hers and drawing her into his arms.

For a moment, he forgot they had an audience. The soft bud of her lips was like a flower that opened at his touch, her mouth sweet like honey, her body pliant in his arms.

For a moment, he disregarded Lady Carwood's aggravating personality. Instead, he enjoyed the memories evoked by the comely woman in his arms, reminders of a time past; a time when he had a woman to warm his bed, set a fire in his loins, and kindle love in his heart.

With a cry, the Highlander thrust Margaret away from him, the look of anguish on his face so fleeting she wondered afterwards if she'd imagined it. But her racing pulse told a different story. *What just happened?* Clenching her fists, Margaret filled her lungs, hoping the deep draught of air would calm her breathing and settle her churning thoughts.

In front of her, Laird Fincastle quickly slipped a mask of impassivity into place, and his jaw tightened as he dropped his head to scan his lines.

Clearing his throat, he returned to the words Bastian had composed for the masque. Green eyes calm now, he touched his chest, then held out his hands. "Ye have my heart, Elizabeth. Keep it safe till we meet again."

Margaret straightened her back, quieting her mind and reverting her focus to the part she had to play. With her heart rate almost back to normal, she put her hands over his, meeting his earnest gaze. "Always."

They stood like that for several seconds, frozen in a tableau, before a shout of, "Bravo!" broke the spell and they sprang apart.

Bastian came towards them, clapping wildly, his face wreathed in smiles. "Bravo!" he repeated, clapping the Highlander on the back. "It appears you *can* act, Laird Fincastle. My faith in you was justified." He stabbed his forefinger at the sheaf of papers in his hand. "Learn your lines, and we will rehearse again tomorrow. Ten o'clock. I'll get the rest of the cast to join us so we can run through every scene. We only have three days till the queen leaves for Stirling, and I want us to be word-perfect by then!"

~

With the others away, the hall quietened, only the crackle of the fire and the dull roar of the wind outside breaking the silence. Settling himself back onto the velvet cushions that softened the hard angles of the window alcove, John pulled a heavy drape across the entrance, shutting out the rest of the world so he could concentrate on Bastian's script.

It would be an honour to play his ancestor, as Lady Carwood had implied. But what man with a brave heart and a modicum of talent could pass up a chance like that? Robert the Bruce had lived a life of legend, and the history the Frenchman had used to create his masque was dramatic and compelling. *However, 'twill not be easy to learn all of these lines by tomorrow. I will have to do naught else.*

Immersed in the stories of The Bruce's wranglings with King Edward of England,

Robert didn't immediately notice that others had entered the hall. And because he was hidden from sight in his window seat, the incomers were also unaware of his presence. It was only when their voices raised in disagreement that John's head jerked up and his attention focussed on the meeting that was taking place beyond his hiding place, rather than the words of the Frenchman's play.

"'Tis the only way," said a gruff voice, a hint of anger evident in his clipped tone.

"Aye." This man's voice was higher-pitched, with the guttural brogue of the north-east. "Her Grace needs rid of him."

John's skin chilled at those words. *They speak of the queen! But who will they be rid of?*

"But not in a way that would harm Prince James' succession." An older man spoke those words, his tone measured and his words precise. "The queen would not allow that."

They must speak of the king! John's breathing quickened.

Yesterday, not long after he had arrived at Craigmillar, John had caught a brief glimpse of Henry Stewart, Lord Darnley, just hours before the king left to ride for Stirling Castle. A cousin of the queen—and probably some distant cousin of John's, since they shared a surname and ancestry dating back to Robert the Bruce—Darnley was tall and handsome, with fair hair and a slim figure.

But his fine looks were deceptive, for the king had gained a reputation as a dissolute drunkard who frequented the taverns and whorehouses of Edinburgh rather than his wife's bed. Even so, could these men really mean to be rid of the *king*? That would be treason at best and regicide at worst.

"The queen would not allow *this*," a more refined voice interjected, his tone nasal, "if she but knew."

"So she must not know," said the older

man again, and paused. "It must be between us, and us alone." Those last words were spoken more slowly, as if he looked each one in the eye.

"You forget the bastard," said the angry one. "'Twas his idea."

"Mmm." John could almost hear the cogs turning in the older man's brain. "But Moray is away right now."

"Conveniently," commented a fifth man with a rich, deep voice John had not heard until now.

They speak of the queen's half-brother. The earl of Moray. If this was a conspiracy, as it appeared to be, John found it hard to believe that Mary's flesh and blood would enter into a plot that impacted her.

"Mayhap. But he will support us in this. He has given his word." There was a creaking of wood, as if the older man sat in one of the oak chairs that surrounded the banqueting tables. "Now, do I have your bond of silence?

For if even a hint gets out, they will have us hanged."

"Or exiled," the refined one sniffed.

The older man drew air through his teeth. "So we must be sure that nobody else knows of our plans."

In the silence that followed, John's nose began to itch, and his eyes started to water as dust from the draperies threatened to make him sneeze. His throat dry, he pinched his nostrils with his left hand, the other hand touching the hilt of his sword. *If they find me, I'm dead,* he thought.

As if to confirm his fear, the next words from the angry lord made John's heart stop.

"If any suspect, they must die." There was a ring of steel as the angry one drew his weapon. "And if any here betray us..." The glint of his sword must have been sufficient threat that he didn't need to finish the sentence.

But John was in agony. The itch in his

nostrils had built to an unbearable pressure, a sneeze imminent and his discovery guaranteed. *I'll have to fight my way out,* he thought, just as the sneeze escaped and all hell broke loose...

Want to find out what happens next?
Order the next book, **A Love Concealed**:

A NOTE ON THE HISTORY

"TRUTH IS STRANGER than fiction, but it is because fiction is obliged to stick to possibilities; truth isn't." Mark Twain

When I started researching Mary Queen of Scots' life, the possibilities for creating dramatic stories leapt out at me. Mary's story reads more like a novel than a non-fiction biography, with spies and plotters around every corner, poisoners and grasping relatives lurking in the shadows, and rebel lords ready to commit murder on more than one occasion to further their cause.

Almost everything you have just read in this story relating to Mary Queen of Scots and Bothwell is true; all I have done is woven the story of two minor characters (Libby and Robert) around those historical events, aiming to show something of the motivations and emotions behind the bald facts of history.

THE HISTORICAL BACKGROUND

Injured while rounding up miscreants for Mary's assizes, Bothwell lay wounded in the forbidding Hermitage Castle. As one of her most loyal supporters and Lieutenant of the Borders, Bothwell was an important member of Mary's Privy Council, and, once the assizes were finished, she rode twenty-five miles to meet with him, returning the same day. But on her way back to Jedburgh, she fell in a bog, and on her return to the town, fell ill.

Initially, it was thought her illness was a mere chill caused by her fall. But over a period of several days she worsened, swooning into unconsciousness and vomiting blood, almost exactly as I've described, until on 26th October 1566 everyone thought she had died. It was only the heroic actions of her surgeon that saved her life.

THE HISTORICAL CHARACTERS IN MY BOOK

Unlike in book one (*A Love Divided*), in this story almost all of the characters existed in history, although some as mere mentions rather than major players.

Our hero and heroine, Robert and Libby, are two of those 'mentions', although Robert does get credited with saving Mary's life by his unconventional treatment of friction &

manipulation, bandaging her limbs and administering an emetic.

Where our hero gave me the biggest headache was in determining his name.

Mary's physicians are recorded variously as Charles Nau, Monsieur Arnault, Monsieur R Nau (which was probably transcribed as Arnault), Arnault Colommius (Columbus?), Jacques Lusgerie, Monsieur Lusury and Dominique Bourgoing. Bourgoing was her last physician, and Lusgerie had attended her from childhood, so there is less contention there. But Claude Nau was the name of the man who wrote Mary's memoirs and was her Secretary from 1575— so was the name Charles Nau a confusion? Or was he Claude's brother (as I read in one source)?

I think it likely that Arnault and Nau were the same person, but which name is correct I am still unsure. However, it seemed likely that Arnault was indeed a transcription of R Nau. So was his first name Charles, or did it start with an 'R'?

In the end, I made the decision on a point of grammar, because writing *Charles'* is much more clumsy than writing *Robert's*, and Robert he became.

HISTORY IS A MYSTERY

Libby's character presented a different issue. She is literally just mentioned by name—Elizabeth Preston—in Mary's household accounts, and that is all I could find out about her.

It's quite likely that Elizabeth Preston was actually related to Simon Preston, owner of Craigmillar Castle (often visited by Mary) and Lord Provost of Edinburgh. Simon's first wife was, in fact, called Elizabeth—Elizabeth Menteith. But in 1540 he married for a second time, so the dates don't add up... *Unless...* I found one source that said Elizabeth was Simon's *second* wife, in which case she might have been the Elizabeth Preston of Mary's household accounts. But one thing I've learned with historical research is to try to find at least three sources in agreement before taking something as fact; and a first marriage in 1540 would've made Simon 30 or 36 years old (again depending on which source for his birthdate is correct), which is a little older than common at that time.

Another option is that Elizabeth Preston was actually Elizabeth *from* Preston, as people in those days were often named after their location or birthplace, and that is the route I decided to take.

In the lowlands of Scotland there are two Preston Towers. One is just a few miles from my home, at Prestonpans on the coast of East Lothian. The other (the one I chose for this story) is near Duns in the Scottish Borders—prime reiver country!

At that time, the holder of Preston Tower

was Robert Logan of Restalrig. But Robert Logan 5th died in 1561 leaving his son, Robert Logan 6th to inherit. There is no record of a daughter, but as women at that time were deemed less important in record-keeping terms, that does not mean that a daughter didn't exist. However, it means that *our* Libby, who would've been sister of Robert 6th, is fictitious.

Agnes Gray, the widow of Robert 5th re-married at some point between 1561 and 1565 to Alexander Home, 5th Lord Home, Warden of the Scottish East March and owner of Hume Castle, which the queen was to visit on her progress through the Borders.

It seemed entirely possible that a senior official such as Lord Home would offer his step-daughter as lady-in-waiting to the queen, so that is the explanation I went with.

SIGNIFICANT DATES

But if there *had* been an Elizabeth from Preston, daughter of Robert Logan and Agnes Gray, the dates don't add up.

Robert 5th is recorded as living from 1533—1561, and marrying Agnes in 1553 (when he'd have been 20).

Agnes is recorded as living from 1540-1581, meaning she'd have married Robert at 13... Unlikely. What is more likely is that her birthdate is wrong (something I've found to be very common), and she was actually born around 1530. Or perhaps the marriage date is wrong, also very common. But either way, if Libby and Robert 6th were born during their parents' marriage, and the marriage date is correct, Libby could have been no older than 13 at the time of our story... so I took some artistic licence there.

But to me, the amazing thing about Mary

Queen of Scots' story is that I had to take *very little* artistic licence.

If you want to see just how little, then can I recommend some further reading?

FURTHER READING

For readers who are interested to know more about Mary Queen of Scots, the best books I've found are:

- *Mary Queen of Scots and the Murder of Lord Darnley* by Alison Weir
- *Mary Queen of Scots* by Antonia Fraser

GLOSSARY

Assizes: A travelling justice court (see Eyres)

Baldrick: A diagonal belt, worn from shoulder to hip, to support a sword

Borders (The Borders): The southern counties of Scotland, adjacent to the border with England

Cramoisie: Crimson/purple

Dirk: Dagger

Doglock rifle: An early firearm

Drove Road: A track used by shepherds and cattle herders to take stock to market

Dwam: To suffer from fainting, giddiness, or be in a stupor

Eyres: A circuit made by an itinerant judge (see Assizes)

Garron: A small, sturdy Scottish pony (see Hobbler)

Gavotte: An old French dance

Glen: A Scottish valley

Glower: An angry or sullen stare

Hand ba': An early fore-runner to rugby or football (soccer)

Hand-fasting: A formal promise of marriage, signified by the joining of hands and making of promises

Hobbler: A small, sturdy Borders pony (see Garron)

Humor: In medieval medicine, doctors thought the body was made up of four fluids or 'humors': blood, phlegm, choler (or yellow bile) and melancholy (or black bile). In a healthy person all four humors were balanced but if you had too much of one you fell ill.

Keep: Castle or tower (see Peel)

Knoll: Hill

Marches: The areas Scotland and England adjacent to the Border. Each country had East, Middle and West Marches

Palfrey: A riding horse particularly suitable for a woman.

Partlet: A woman's garment covering the neck and shoulders, worn especially during the 16th century

Posset: A warm drink of wine and curdled milk

Privy Council: A body of advisers appointed by the sovereign

Reiver: A thieving rider

Sack: A sweet wine fortified with brandy (known today as sherry)

Saut buckie: The Salt Box - a recess, usually beside a fireplace, where salt was stored to keep it dry

Sot: Drunkard, alcoholic

Tup: A male sheep

Turnpike (stair): A spiral staircase

Warden (of the Marches): Official in charge of dispensing justice in the Borderlands (see Day of Truce)

CHARACTERS

Names in **bold** are real historical characters.

Alexander, Lord Home: warden of the Scottish East March

Alexandra Graham: Daughter of Simon and heiress to Kersdale Keep

Claude Nau: French lawyer. Robert's half-brother

Édouard McMann: Du Croc's Secretary

George Gordon, 5th Earl of Huntly

George Seton, 7th Lord Seton: half-brother of

Mary Seton and Master of the Queen's household

Henry, Lord Scrope: Warden of the English West March

Henry Stewart, Lord Darnley: Mary's husband and cousin

Hugh, Master of Somerville: eldest son and heir of Lord Somerville

Black Jack Heron: English reiver from the East March

Jacques Lusgerie: chief physician to Mary Queen of Scots

James Hepburn, Earl of Bothwell: Member of Mary's Privy Council and Lieutenant of the Borders

James Stewart, Earl of Moray: Mary's half-brother, illegitimate son of James V, member of her Privy Council

Lady Jean Gordon: Bothwell's wife and Huntly's sister

Little Jock Elliot of the Park: Notorious reiver

*Libby (**Elizabeth**) Logan of **Preston***: Lady-in-Waiting to Mary Queen of Scots

Mary Beaton (Beth): Lady-in-Waiting to Mary Queen of Scots

Mary Fleming (Flam): Lady-in-Waiting to Mary Queen of Scots

Mary Livingston (Livvy): Lady-in-Waiting to Mary Queen of Scots

Mary Seton (Ebba): Lady-in-Waiting to Mary Queen of Scots

Mary Stuart, Queen of Scots

Michael Cranstoun: Deputy Warden of the Scottish Middle March, laird of Penchrise and Master of Stobs Castle

Nicholas Hubert, 'French Paris': Bothwell's page

Philibert Du Croc (Monsieur du Croc): The French ambassador

*Robert **Nau***: French doctor. Physician to the French ambassador

Iron Simon Graham: Alex's father, Lord of Kersdale

Sir Thomas Kerr, Laird of Ferniehirst

William Maitland of Lethington: Mary's Secretary

ABOUT THE AUTHOR

A native Scot who lives in the hinterland between Edinburgh and the Borders, Belle loves to write about Scotland and its history.

In addition to writing historical romance, she rides dressage, teaches skiing - and pens prize-winning sci-fi, urban fantasy and contemporary romance as Roz Marshall books2read.com/rl/RozMarshall, and cozy mysteries as R.B. Marshall books2read.com/rl/RBMarshall

Find out more about Belle and her upcoming books by joining her newsletter: subscribepage.com/joinbelle

ALSO BY

BY BELLE MCINNES:

Mary's Ladies *series [complete]*

Sweet/clean Scottish Historical Romance telling the story of Mary Queen of Scots:

- *A Love Divided*
- *A Love Beyond*
- *A Love Concealed*
- *A Love Departed*

The Macrae Legends *series*

Clean Scottish Historical Romance telling of the beginnings of Clan Macrae, during the time of William Wallace and Robert the Bruce:

- *For Love or Justice* (releasing 31 Aug 2021)

BY BELLE MCINNES, WRITING AS R.B MARSHALL:

The **Highland Horse Whisperer** series

Cozy Mystery set in Scotland (and London for the prequel):

- *The Secret Santa Mystery*
- *A Corpse at the Castle*
- *A Right Royal Revenge*
- *A Poisoning at the Pageant (due in 2021)*
- *Henchman at the Highland Games (due in 2022)*

BY BELLE MCINNES, WRITING AS ROZ MARSHALL:

The **Celtic Fey** series

Urban Fantasy / Young Adult Fantasy set in Scotland (and the faerie realm):

- *Unicorn Magic*
- *Kelpie Curse*
- *Faerie Quest*
- *The Fey Bard*
- *Wizard's Potion*
- *Merlin's Army* (releasing 30 May 2o21)

Secrets in the Snow series

Women's Fiction / Sweet Sports Romance set in a Scottish ski school:

- *Fear of Falling*
- *My Snowy Valentine*
- *The Racer Trials*
- *Snow Blind*
- *Weathering the Storm*

Half Way Home stories

Young Adult Science Fiction set in Hugh Howey's *Half Way Home* universe:

- *Nobody's Hero*
- *The Final Solution*

Scottish stories:

- *Still Waters*

BIBLIOGRAPHY

Ball, Krista D. *What Kings Ate and Wizards Drank*

Bingham, Madeleine. *Scotland Under Mary Stuart - an Account of Everyday Life*

Colburn, H, (1842) *Letters of Mary, Queen of Scots: And Documents Connected with Her Personal History*

Coventry, Martin. *The Castles of Scotland*

Crisp, Peter. *Clothes: Tudors and Stuarts*

Fraser, Antonia. *Mary Queen of Scots*

Fraser, George MacDonald. *The Steel Bonnets*

Hale, John. *Mary Queen of Scots*

BIBLIOGRAPHY

Hermitage Castle, Official Guide (Historic Scotland)

In Search of the Border Reivers (map by Ordnance Survey)

Knox, John. *History of the Reformation in Scotland, Volume Two*

MacNalty, Sir Arthur, K.C.B. *The Maladies of Mary Queen of Scots*

Mahon, R.H., Major-General. *Mary Queen of Scots, a study of the Lennox Narrative*

Marshall, Rosalind K. *Queen Mary's Women*

Mary was Here: Where Mary Queen of Scots went and what she did there (Historic Scotland)

Mayhew, Mickey. *The Little Book of Mary Queen of Scots*

Mikhaila, Ninya & Malcolm-Davies, Jane. *The Tudor Tailor: Reconstructing sixteenth-century dress*

Moffat, Alistair. *The Reivers*

Musgrave, Thea. *Mary, Queen of Scots: An Opera in Three Acts*

Nau, Claude. *The History of Mary Stewart:*

From the Murder of Riccio Until Her Flight Into England

Oddy, Zilla. *Mary Queen of Scots' House, Jedburgh: A Look at the Building and Its Inhabitants*

Pease, Howard. *The Lord Wardens of the Marches of England and Scotland*

Pocket Scottish History: story of a nation (Lomond)

Ross, David. *Scotland: History of a Nation*

Schiern, Frederik. *Life of James Hepburn, Earl of Bothwell*

Small, John. *Queen Mary at Jedburgh in 1566*

Thomson, Thomas (1768-1852). *Diurnal of Occurrents - from a manuscript of the sixteenth century*

Stedall, Robert. *The Challenge to the Crown, Vol 1*

Weir, Alison. *Mary Queen of Scots and the Murder of Lord Darnley*

Many web articles and wikipedia entries

www.ingramcontent.com/pod-product-compliance
Lightning Source LLC
Chambersburg PA
CBHW010548170726
48285CB00011B/2806